Fly Free

Award-winning author C.
educated in New York City
three grown-up sons. She
York State.

C. S. Adler

FLY FREE

Piper Books
in association with Heinemann

For the best of mothers, mine

Acknowledgements

Thanks for information provided by Sue Clark,
benefactor of raptors, and
Geraldine Foster, teacher and wildlife lover.

First published in Great Britain in 1988 by William Heinemann Ltd
This Piper edition published in 1989 by Pan Books Ltd,
Cavaye Place, London SW10 9PG
in association with William Heinemann
9 8 7 6 5 4 3 2 1
© C. S. Adler 1984
ISBN 0 330 30901 3

Printed and bound in Great Britain by
Courier International Limited, Tiptree, Essex

This book is sold subject to the condition that it
shall not by way of trade or otherwise, be lent, re-sold,
hired out, or otherwise circulated without the publisher's prior
consent in any form of binding or cover other than that in which
it is published and without a similar condition including this
condition being imposed on the subsequent purchaser

One

Charlotte's voice startled Shari out of her daydream and nearly caused her to fall out of the tree.

"What are you doing up there? And why aren't you watching your little brother? I got to leave, and you better find him fast if you know what's good for you," Charlotte said.

Shari looked down into her mother's anger-flushed face and was tempted to retreat to higher branches, but deliberately disobeying Charlotte was too risky. Instead, Shari swung down from her seat in the notch between the trunk and the thick lower limb that jutted halfway across the backyard. She landed lightly beyond Charlotte's striking range.

"Big girl like you hanging about in trees like an ape. You ought to be ashamed of yourself," Charlotte said. "Shari Ape Face, that's what I'm calling you from now on. Well, where's Peter?"

"I'll get him," Shari said and started off, anxious to get away before Charlotte asked again where he was, and Shari had to admit that she'd let him go to Mabel's store by himself.

Peter was six and would waste his spending money on

what Charlotte considered junk—cheap sweets and toys from the bubble-gum machine. But this morning, he had told Shari earnestly, "I got to go alone. I'm a big boy now, and I got a right to go alone." Shari sympathized with his need for independence. Being five years younger than any other child in the family made it hard for him to grow up. Also, she knew that he didn't want her along today because he intended to buy her a belated birthday present. He'd been saving up for it. Usually he confided his plans to her before they could even qualify as secrets, but this time he hadn't. "You'll see," he had said. "I'm getting you something good."

Something to do with birds, she expected. He knew how much she loved birds. Last year, for her twelfth birthday, he'd given her a fluffy polyester chicken with a plastic beak and legs, not her ideal bird image, but she treasured it because it came from him. He was her special brother, her "pair partner". Everyone in their family paired off. It was their mother, Charlotte, with their father, Zeke, then Doug and Walter, the two brothers who'd been born right after Shari and who were now twelve and eleven. She'd been odd man out until Peter came along six years ago.

Shari ran the quarter of a mile along the shoulder of the highway to Mabel's store. She called to Peter as soon as she got close enough to see him. He was talking to a boy more her age than his, who was slouched against the scarred clapboard siding of Mabel's store. The boy had a sneer on his face that made Shari wish Peter were not such a wag-tail puppy of a boy that he would try to make friends with just about anybody.

"Peter," she called again, but still he didn't hear her. No surprise in that. Shari was always being told by teachers to speak up, but she couldn't do it. Quietness was part of her protective camouflage.

"My sister can," Peter was saying. "She could jump from this old roof to the shed easy."

"I'll bet," the mean-eyed stranger mocked. "Even a boy would need wings to jump that far."

"My sister can jump better than any boy. She can climb trees too, and she can even walk across a rope if it's tight enough."

"This your sister?" the kid asked.

Peter turned and saw her. A grin rounded his pudgy cheeks. "Shari, this kid don't believe me. You tell him. You can jump that far, can't you?"

"I don't know." She had no interest in proving anything to the unpleasant-looking stranger. All she wanted was to get Peter home before Charlotte got too angry. "Ma's been looking for you, Petey."

"I bet you couldn't even climb to the top of a roof that steep, let alone jump across to that shed," the kid taunted.

"Show him, Shari," Peter begged. "Show him how easy you can do it, please!"

"She sent me to get you. She wants you home *now*," Shari said. No need to spell it out for him. Little as he was, he understood who would suffer if he didn't leave immediately.

She saw an uncertain flicker in his eyes, but he protested. "It'll only take you a minute. Come on. Show

3

him, Shari."

Five minutes, she estimated and was tempted. She loved to climb and jump. It was as close to flying as she could get. The steep shingled roof of Mabel's general store would be easy enough to clamber up in trainers, but jumping to the low shed off to one side could be tricky. She'd need a running start to clear the four or five feet of space between. While Shari considered, Peter said to her, "Guess who this kid's visiting, Shari?"

"I'm visiting my great aunt," the boy got in quickly, as if to ward off insult. "She lives back there." He jerked his head towards the run-down house across the highway and down in a hollow where the duck lady lived. There, hordes of noisy white ducks quacked around a pond behind the feather-strewn fence that protected them from the wheels of the trucks that sped past night and day.

"I'll do the jump after lunch," Shari decided.

"I'll be gone by then," the boy said. "My dad and me got to get to Burlington. But that's okay. I figured you couldn't do it. It'd take a circus guy, a trapeze artist, to jump that far."

"Shari could be in a circus if she wanted," Peter said.

"I can do it," she said impulsively. This was the closest to being a flyer she was ever likely to get.

Peter radiated with pride, as if she'd already proven his boast, when she began to shinny up the drainpipe. No sooner did she reach the roof than she forgot him. She had this moment all to herself, the thrill of feeling her pliable, narrow body behave as if she were made of elastic instead of bones and muscle. She ran lightly up to the ridgepole and balanced there for a few seconds, breathing deeply of the pine- and juniper-scented Vermont woods spread out in great curves on the hillsides around her. She could taste summer in the wind as she looked back up the road to her own diminutive house tucked into the hillside. The giant green head of her favourite tree reared up behind her house, and near it lay the rusty car that Zeke still hadn't had time between long-distance truck hauls to fix for Charlotte. To the left below the duck pond, where a narrow road traced a thin line, the steeple of the Methodist church poked through surrounding greenery. If she were a bird, she would swoop from this roof down over the steeple and cruise over the lake where Zeke sometimes took them swimming when he was home long enough in the summers. If she were a bird, if only—

"You gonna jump or just take in the view?" the boy asked, squinting up at her.

The distance to the shed looked greater than it had seemed from below. Rusty nails stained the ragged asphalt shingles. Dark patches made her wonder how sturdy the shed roof was. If she broke through, Charlotte would make her pay for it. "Are you a girl or a monkey?" Charlotte might ask. And how could Shari pay Mabel for damaging her roof when she hadn't even been able to save enough money to replace the parakeet that her father had given her which had flown out of her open bedroom window last summer?

Shari hesitated, but before she could change her mind, Peter urged, "Jump, Shari." And from down the road came Charlotte's shrill voice calling her name. Shari started. She hunched into herself, then backed up and sprinted along the ridgepole. She flew across the space between the two buildings. Her arm reached towards the shed, and she felt the joy of being suspended in air. For those seconds, she was a hawk soaring on wind currents high above the shirred green mountainsides, light and free and wholly beautiful. Then the palms of her hands took the abrasive blow of the landing. She did a forward roll so that she wound up with her weight evenly distributed, stretched out lightly on her back on the shed roof.

"See? Did you see that?" Peter was chortling down below. "My sister can climb and jump better than anybody."

Instantly she eased herself over to the edge and jumped to the ground. "We've got to get going, Peter. Don't you hear her?" She grabbed Peter's hand and began running, blind to the open-mouthed admiration of the stranger. All that mattered now was reaching Charlotte before she exploded.

Peter chugged along behind Shari, clinging to the cardboard tube he'd bought at Mabel's store and panting. He wasn't much of a runner. As Zeke said, it was Peter's mouth that ran best.

"We showed him, didn't we show him?" Peter said between gasps for breath when they reached the kitchen door of their house.

"Why do you care what that boy thought? He wasn't anything to you."

"No, he was just a big blabbermouth, nothing but a big old blabbermouth, but we showed him anyway," Peter insisted. Her thirteen-year-old wisdom bounced right off his rubber-skinned consciousness of the world. It frustrated her when she couldn't make him see things the way she did, but she had no time to try again before Charlotte whipped the screen door open and confronted them.

"Well, you sure took your time getting here. I went down to the road and couldn't find you. Where were you?" Anger swelled the edges of her still-girlish prettiness so that she didn't look like the beauty queen Zeke claimed she could be.

"I got about the best-looking wife in Vermont," Zeke always said of Charlotte, "and sweet as Vermont's maple syrup too." Shari wondered how he'd see her if he stayed at home with her more; but the trucking company he worked for kept him on the road most of the time, especially during the summer months when so much produce was harvested and shipped.

"Didn't I tell you I got to get my hair done this afternoon?" Charlotte said. "Think just because BeeJay is my friend it don't matter when I show up? You know it's not polite to be late for an appointment. You know she's got a business to run, and they're doing me a favour already having Marvin pick me up on his way back to the shop from lunch. A lot you care about anything I got to do. What were you doing? Swinging in the trees again, Miss Shari Lally, ape girl? And how did you cut yourself?"

Shari looked down at her hands. The right one was bleeding—from a nail on the shed roof probably. "I'll get a plaster," Shari said.

"Put iodine on it. And Peter, you eat something quick. I'm taking you with me. You're going to the dental clinic today."

"Do I have to?" Peter asked. He was carefully pouring himself a glass of milk from the container in the refrigerator. Shari could see him as she reached for a plaster in the cabinet in the bathroom, which was next to the back door.

A car honked, a double beep of command from the road outside their house. The car couldn't take refuge in the drive because Peter's hand-me-down fleet of dump trucks and lorries and cranes littered the tarmac there. Charlotte cursed and ran to the living-room window to wave at Marvin, then dashed back to tell Peter, "Forget that milk. You got no time to eat now."

"But I'm hungry!" Peter protested. His good nature depended on regular and frequent feedings. When hungry, Peter whined.

"Grab a banana and let's go," Charlotte said. "Shari, I told you to get his toys out of the drive, didn't I? Now why can't you ever do like I ask you? People could get killed stopping on the road because they can't use our drive the way it's junked up with stuff. You get it cleared out by the time I get back or else. And don't forget the washing." She dashed out of the front door, hauling Peter behind her and leaving the screen door wide open.

The peace of the empty house settled around Shari like balm. She felt sorry for her brother. Right now he'd be whimpering from hunger in the car between Charlotte and the gossipy Marvin, who co-owned the Shear and

8

Shave Hair Cutting Parlour with his sister BeeJay. Shari hoped BeeJay or someone took pity on Peter and bought him a snack.

She drank the glass of milk he'd left and considered whether to make a baloney sandwich or her usual peanut butter. She didn't feel much like either. "Skinny as a wet cat," Charlotte called her, when she wasn't comparing Shari to an ape. "At your age I'd been wearing a bra for years." The comment had lacked the barb Charlotte had intended because Shari liked her narrow, supple body. She still daydreamed of being an Indian girl, invisible in the woods, at one with the lean trunks of the reeds, as long and straight as her dark brown hair. She practised disappearing in classrooms too. There she sat silent and motionless, answering questions in a whisper so that teachers forgot her existence. Hers was usually the last name they learned, and Shari preferred it that way.

She wandered out of the front door to consider the drive her mother had told her to clear. Peter had dug a hole in the soft dirt where the tarmac had cracked apart. He had certainly made a mess.

She wished she could let everything stay where it was and steal an hour along on the mountain for herself. It would be fun to explore that spot where the water bubbled up through bare rock, ice cold even on the hottest summer day. Above that was a ledge, too difficult for Peter to climb, where she could sit and dangle her legs and contemplate the world below, so peaceful in its distance. No sense even thinking about it. To have escaped Charlotte's wrath this noon had been miracle enough for one day.

Abruptly Shari got to work. She piled the trucks in an empty carton under the carport. Doug and Walter hadn't shown up for lunch. She supposed they'd taken sandwiches along to their vegetable stand by the crossroads so that they wouldn't have to lose any sales by biking home before supper time. That would be Doug's idea. He was so intent on making money this summer that he didn't even take the time out for the ball games which used to be his whole life. As for Walter, he went along with whatever interested Doug, content so long as he could keep a book in his pocket and spend most of his time reading it.

The drive looked fine when Shari finished. She was hot from working in the sun, so she climbed into her shaggy-leafed tree, up to the notch that fitted her body like a contoured chair. Walter and Doug used this spot as a hiding place sometimes. They would shoot their peashooters or water guns from here. But mostly the tree was her place. Here she could relax into the airy sensations of sun and shadow, entertained by the warblers and the twits and tweets of chickadees. The trickling sweetness of time flowing by began to refresh her spirit as always.

She remembered the washing when it was too late. The slam of the car door and Charlotte's double-pronged laugh jolted Shari. Mid-afternoon, judging by the sun's position. They were back before she'd expected them.

"Shari, where are you?" Charlotte called. Her hair was set in frosted waves fixed with hair spray that she would not brush out for days. Shari liked Charlotte's hair best when rain made it curl in a fluffy cloud around her face. Shari liked her own reedlike body and didn't mind the pencilled-on look of her features, but she wished she'd inherited her mother's hair. It was the only part of Charlotte she wished was hers.

In the kitchen, Shari saw the cardboard tube Peter had carried back from Mabel's store lying near the wall where everybody's muddy shoes and winter boots were dropped. She picked the tube up.

"That's your present. You didn't look at it yet, did you?" Peter asked as he trailed in after Charlotte, who went to look at her hair in the mirror in the bathroom.

"This is for me?" Shari asked, trying to sound surprised.

"I told you I was gonna get you a good present, but I didn't have enough money before. It's that poster with a bird on it."

"You mean the one with the hawk over the valley?"

"That's the one. You said you liked it."

"It's my most favourite. Oh, Peter, I can't believe you really got it for me."

"Well, I did." He beamed as he urged her to open it.

Charlotte came out of the bathroom and listened to Shari exclaiming over what a wonderful present the poster was, and how she didn't mind at all that it was three weeks late. The more fuss she made, the happier Peter looked.

"What'd you do about the washing?" Charlotte asked.

"I did the drive," Shari said.

"Big deal. That took you about two minutes—"

"A lady at BeeJay's gave me a sugar bun," Peter interrupted, "and I didn't have to go to the dentist either, because the sign on the door said it was closed. And we drove past Walter and Doug. Boy, are they making lots of money! There was six cars at their stand."

"I'm going in to watch my soap," Charlotte said as if she were bored with the whole exchange. "And maybe I'll take a nap before dinner. You keep Peter out of the house, will you? You can do the washing later."

Shari couldn't believe her luck. Charlotte had given her a gift of sun-gilded hours in the woods. "Peter," Shari whispered, "let's hang up the poster tonight and go down to the stream and pan for gold now, okay?"

"Yeah," Peter said, his eyes widening with delight. Panning for gold excited him more than just paddling around in the stream with her. It was one of the tricks she used to make the things she liked appealing to him.

Shari grabbed the sifter from under the scraggy forsythia bush, now summer green instead of spring golden.

"You going to borrow Mama's sifter again? She'll kill you, Shari," Peter said.

"I'll put up my invisible shield."

"But it didn't work last time."

"Sometimes I don't get it out in time."

"I don't like it when she hits you," Peter complained.

"Don't worry. She can't hurt me." Saying it helped her to believe it. Besides, going around scared all the time just spoiled the sweetness of the good moments, the free time when she could fly. As for the sifter, Shari needed it to keep Peter busy. He liked using equipment, whether in the soft dirt at the edge of the drive or in the sandy bottom of the stream.

They walked one behind the other on the ill-defined path to the ravine where a stream rushed madly over fallen debris in spring, but was tame now in summer. This late in the afternoon, the bottom of the ravine was already shadowed in for evening.

"Maybe we should pan for gold tomorrow," Peter said cautiously.

"Come on; it's not that dark," she pleaded. "We'll only stay an hour."

He shrugged, already too old to own up to being scared. A year ago he would have, but he was tired of Doug taunting him for being the baby and anxious to catch up with his older brothers. "You go ahead and I'll follow," he told Shari. "I can get down okay by myself."

It was true. Going down, he relied on his bottom for security. It was on the climb up that he always hung on to some part of Shari as she guided them from rock to tree root to bush and he looked up fearfully at how far they still had to climb. He never looked back. She had convinced him not to.

Peter slid the last ten feet on his blue-jeaned bottom getting well coated with the mud at the edge of the stream. Shari made a mental note to rinse his jeans off with the garden hose before entering the kitchen. Charlotte took it as a personal attack if they tracked mud into the house. Last week when Peter had brought a turtle home, along with muddy grass, rocks and moss for its tank, Charlotte's punishing hand had lashed out quicker than

Shari could duck. On her mother's orders, Shari had released the turtle in their backyard. But Peter sniffled and wept all through supper, until Charlotte finally relented and sent Shari to retrieve the creature. Walter and Doug had helped her search, but the turtle had made its escape for good. Peter had cried himself to sleep.

"Don't say I didn't try to get it back for you," Charlotte had said to him in the morning. "Maybe I'll get you some goldfish instead." She didn't, though. Charlotte disliked animals.

Peter squatted beside the stream with the sieve at the ready. "We can keep the gold if we find it, can't we?"

"Sure," Shari said. "This is our own place, Peter. Nobody comes here but us. Whatever we find is ours."

"Fishermen come though."

"Only on the other side of the bridge, across the road, never here."

"And there's really gold?"

"Doesn't it look just like the picture I showed you in the library book where they were prospecting for gold in California?"

"Yes, but then why's nobody found any yet?"

"Because nobody but us has looked. Now concentrate." He set to work sieving the streambed as Shari's eyes followed a brown bird in the undergrowth. She wondered what it was after in there—insects, seeds, material to line its nest? She could hear it skittering about, but couldn't see it any more. If she were that bird, manoeuvring through the bushes—but it would have problems too, she thought. No way to escape them.

The burbling water hurried around rocks and logs and made sharp little rills before settling over deeper pools. A crow flapped from one side of the ravine to the other. Did it mind their presence? She had found a nest of cardinals last spring and had watched them raise their young, even witnessing the last baby's first flight. But when she tried to write about it for a school composition, it hadn't come out sounding nearly like the thrill it had been. The kind of joys she had were hard to share.

She was a person who liked being alone. At school, when she had a choice between working by herself or with a partner, she chose to work alone. Then she would finish quickly and use the leftover time to daydream or to sit back as if she were at a play and watch the others flirting and teasing and tormenting one another. All their fighting, note passing and tricks were interesting to observe, but she resisted any attempt to get her to participate. Her classmates knew she was a swift runner, good at gymnastics, and that she was quiet. They knew her name and that was enough. Total anonymity would have suited her better.

Once Shari's third-grade teacher, determined to wean her from her shyness, had given her a speaking part in a school play. She'd whispered her way through rehearsals, but the teacher wouldn't relent. Dressed as a fairy godmother on the day of the performance, with both her parents in the audience, Shari had been unable to utter a word.

"You embarrassed us to death, acting like a dummy in front of the whole school," Charlotte had scolded in the car on the way home.

Then Zeke had attempted to comfort Shari. "Don't feel so bad, baby," he said. "You looked mighty cute in your costume, and everybody got the idea without your saying anything anyway." He squeezed her shoulder, but couldn't lessen her humiliation.

Nobody else in the family liked the things she liked or enjoyed being alone. Even Zeke, who had to spend long hours on the road in the cab of his truck by himself, said he depended on his C.B. radio, not just to keep in touch with other drivers for safety's sake, but for company. And if BeeJay, Charlotte's closest friend, was busy, Charlotte would summon Lina, whom she called "that boring potato sack" behind her back, to keep her company. If no one came to visit and Zeke wasn't home, Charlotte went to bed when her children did and left the TV on so that she could hear human voices in the house all night. The woods that attracted Shari frightened Charlotte.

Slowly, Peter and Shari worked their way downstream to the narrowest part of the ravine, where the wrecked car of the robbers still lay with doors sprung open and front end crushed in. The police had chased the teenage robbers until their car had careered off the road above and torn a wayward path down the bare slope into the ravine. The boys had been lucky to escape alive.

"Tell me again how we'll spend the gold, Shari," Peter asked. Talk, even talk he had heard before, suited him better than the subtle song of the birds and wind and water.

"I told you," she said. "First thing we do after we stake our claim is get out a big bucket of gold nuggets and take it to the bank and open a savings account. Then we'll lend Zeke enough money so he can quit truck driving and buy a little business for Charlotte and him to work in together."

"And I get a two wheeler."

"The best two wheeler we can find, and those cowboy boots you wanted for last Christmas besides."

"And an air-gun."

"Not yet. You're too young."

"And all the video games and my own TV."

"Yes."

"And you get a bird, Shari, a green one like Chirpy was."

"Blue this time," she said. "I could call him Starlight, or Blue Boy maybe." Her voice snagged on a memory that still had the power to hurt her. She looked at the uncompromising rocks, willing them to turn golden, and swallowed and said, "I'm going to buy a plane, too, a little one I can learn to fly by myself." That was her latest dream, replacement for her old desire to be magically transformed into a bird.

"You are?" He sounded alarmed. She had never told him that before.

"What's wrong with a plane?" she asked. "Wouldn't you like it if I became a jet pilot?"

"I don't want you to fly away from here."

"What makes you think I'd do that?"

"Because?"

"I won't leave you, Petey Pie. You don't have to worry," she promised.

He hugged her then, muddy hands and all. Except for Zeke, Peter was the only one who ever hugged her. Charlotte would sometimes take Peter onto her lap and cuddle him, but Shari couldn't remember the last time she and her mother had hugged or kissed.

To get to the wrecked car, they had to cross the stream above the rapids where water thundered down even in summer. A tree straddled the stream conveniently, but one slip from its narrow trunk and the next landing could be on the rocks below the first six-foot drop. As usual, Peter squeezed his eyes shut and swore he wouldn't cross. As usual, Shari ran lightly across and back to show him how easy it was. Next she took his cold hands and coaxed him forward inch by inch as she backed across the log, as steady as if she were walking on level ground. She didn't forget to tell him how brave he was when they reached the other side.

"It's getting dark," he answered fretfully. "And I'm hungry."

"Not yet. A little longer," she pleaded, reluctant to return to the kitchen where Charlotte would soon be standing by the stove with a cigarette dangling from her sulky mouth as she cooked their dinner.

A catbird warbled throatily, then twittered an imitation of another bird's song as it bounced on a springy twig above them. "Listen to that, Peter," she said to distract him. "Doesn't that little grey bird sing better than anybody?"

The running brook chimed sedately, now that they'd left the falls behind. Leaves hummed wind lullabies. Feeling happy, Shari followed the slanted sun rays to where the carcass of the robbers' car lay like a crushed animal, its nose to the stream edge. Something glinted in the tangle of weeds there. She bent and picked up a large chunk of glass. When she washed it in the stream, she caught her breath as the sleek, curved neck of a swan with swept-back wings emerged. "Petey, look what I found."

"Gold?" he asked.

"Almost." The smooth weight of the bird nestled on her palm as if it belonged there as she showed it to him.

"Is it a treasure?"

"*I* think so." She set it in his cupped hands. "Isn't it marvellous, Petey?"

"No," he answered honestly. "It's just a glass bird."

"But it's so beautiful," she said, "and it's not chipped or scratched or anything." She took the swan back into her own hands, and again it fitted into her palm and warmed into life as she held it. "I think it's something precious."

"Can we sell it and get rich?" Peter asked.

"I'd rather keep it," she said. She held the bird against her cheek and closed her eyes. "I never owned anything this pretty," she murmured. Not the stone with the red grains that might be garnets, not the butterfly pin without a back that Peter had found and given her, nor the feather from the tail of the green parakeet who'd disappeared into the woods last summer. Nothing had ever come into her hands as lovely as this graceful bird.

Peter's stomach rumbled out loud. "I'm starving," he complained. "And it's getting really dark down here."

"We'll go," she said apologetically. He hadn't eaten much for lunch today. She took him by one hand, carefully holding the swan in the other, and began immediately to lead him home.

Two

After the grey and brown halftones of the ravine, the lemony gleam of the late afternoon made Shari and Peter blink. Only when they reached their own backyard, where the mountainside blocked the last slanted sun rays and turned tree trunks into black pillars, did they find evening again. Peter hurried towards the lighted window of their kitchen, eager for the comforts of food and family awaiting him inside, but Shari hung back. For her, the glowing square of window was like an open fire, both attraction and threat.

The car in their drive belonged to Charlotte's friend Lina. When Lina's husband went on the road with his sample case, she often dropped in to "visit awhile" and stayed on through supper if Charlotte's need for company was great enough to allow that. Lina would sit placidly clucking in sympathy while Charlotte talked at a fast trot. What she told the childless, bulky Lina was the latest edition of old news—how Charlotte wished Zeke made more money so they could afford some item Charlotte desired, and how lonely she got with him gone all the time, and what rotten luck she had being stuck in the country with four kids to drive her up the wall. After

Lina left, Charlotte would complain that entertaining that woman gave her a headache, but she couldn't be too choosy about her friends here in the middle of nowheresville.

Tonight, as Shari lingered outside the door, she heard her mother going on again about how she'd planned a career in fashion, had an eye for it and could have become a buyer if she hadn't married Zeke and become pregnant instead.

"No fashion career around here, that's for sure," Lina agreed.

"I'll say. And Zeke don't want me to work anyway. Remember when I took that job as hostess in the Blue Hill Hotel? And Zeke got so mad at me I had to quit? Of course, the place only lasted one summer anyway, but what got Zeke was he thought the owner had his eye on me."

"Maybe he did," Lina said. "You don't look like the mother of four kids."

"No, I've kept my figure. I can eat whatever I want and never put on weight."

"Well, you burn it up with nerves. Nervous energy burns up fat. Take me. Not a nerve in my body. Everything I put in my mouth just stays with me." She patted her lumpy thighs as if she were proud of them.

"I bet you eat more than you think you do, Lina."

They argued mildly about that for a minute, and then Charlotte said, "Where's that sister of yours, Pete? She stuck up in a tree somewhere?"

"She's coming," Peter said. "Ma, can I have a can of

spaghetti? I'm hungry."

"Don't bother me now. Can't you see I'm talking with Lina? Go watch some TV until your brothers get home.... That Shari. People say it's good getting the girl first so she can help out with the younger kids, but Shari don't do a thing around this house unless I'm right on her tail to make her."

"Don't she take care of her little brother all the time?" Lina said. "You got to give her credit for that."

"Credit? What for? She don't mind having him follow her around like a puppy. And who else is going to pay attention to her? She don't have a friend her own age. Now I ask you, Lina, is that normal? A girl her age so shy she can't even open her mouth in school."

"But she does all right in school anyway, don't she?"

"Well, sure. She's smart enough. All my kids are smart."

"That's not so great for you, Charlotte," Lina said. "That just means you got to figure on paying their way through college."

"We're not sending these kids to college, not on what Zeke makes," Charlotte said. "Besides, Walter's the only one who likes school, and he can just win himself a scholarship if he wants to go. You can bet Doug's not going to waste four more years in some classroom when he can be out working. He'll probably be making a fortune by the time he's old enough for college. You know what he told me the other night? 'Mama,' he said, 'when I'm rich, I'm going right out and buy you a new car.' That's what he said."

"What about Shari?" Lina asked.

"Oh. Shari. She'll get married like I did, or else end up cleaning out motel rooms or waiting tables."

"She could be a teacher or something," Lina said.

"Shari? Don't make me laugh. She couldn't get her mouth to open to a stranger to save her life."

"Shari wants to be a pilot," Peter's voice piped up defensively. "She wants to fly jet planes."

"Fly? Where'd she get a notion like that?" Charlotte said sharply with a note of fear in her voice. She paused, then said, "Anyways, you got to go to school to be a pilot, and Shari's going to work as soon as she finishes high school."

"What about you, Charlotte?" Lina said. "You could find a job."

"I could, huh? Doing what?"

"Sales clerk in the shopping mall maybe."

"Oh, sure. They're just waiting to hire a housewife with no experience, and besides, how am I going to drive forty minutes each way when there's ice and snow on the roads and my car don't run half the time? Think I haven't thought about that mall? But until I get a car that works right, forget it."

"Yeah, well, working is not all it's cracked up to be anyway. Who wants to get up and get dressed early every morning?" Lina said. "Me, I'm so glad I can just roll over and sleep as long as I like."

"That's because you're lazy, Lina. I'm not lazy. . . . Where *is* that girl? Mooning around in the woods somewhere?" Charlotte said angrily. Being with Lina always made her irritable after a while. "That girl's never around to help me. All she thinks about is herself."

"It's funny," Lina said, "how the boys are the spitting image of Zeke and Shari don't look like you nor him."

"She takes after Zeke's family," Charlotte said, and added, "Listen, if you're not staying for dinner, I better start getting something for the kids. The boys are going to be hungry working that produce stand all day."

Lina ignored the hint. Her pillowlike nature seemed immune to insult. "Don't mind me. I'll just sit here and watch you work. I never mind watching someone else work."

"It makes me nervous to be watched," Charlotte said. "It was nice that you dropped by, Lina. I'll walk you to your car."

The sound of a chair scraping on the vinyl floor was followed by the slower sounds of Lina rising reluctantly to leave.

Shari took a deep breath. When Zeke got home, she would have to ask him if it was true that you had to go to school to become a pilot. She didn't want to clean motel rooms or wait on tables for a living.

As Charlotte ushered Lina out of the front door, Shari slipped into the kitchen. She began setting the table immediately so that her mother couldn't find any fault with her.

"So, you finally got home," Charlotte said when she returned. "Where were you all this time?"

"Just outside."

The back door burst open and Doug and Walter piled

in. Doug dropped into a chair at the kitchen table. He lay on the chair like a plank, with his head on the back and his legs stuck straight out, just the way Zeke did. "Boy, am I beat. When are we going to eat?" Doug said.

Walter was gulping water from the kitchen tap.

"I haven't started dinner yet, so don't bug me," Charlotte answered. "How about if I open a couple of cans of spaghetti?"

"Not again, Ma," Doug said.

"Well, don't blame me. You can't expect me to get to the supermarket without a car."

"We got some tomatoes and marrow we didn't sell that's only a little bruised," Walter said. "Don't we have any hamburger meat?"

Charlotte shrugged and went to the refrigerator.

"You going to take us to the bank so we can make a deposit soon?" Doug asked.

"I'll try and get BeeJay or Marvin to give you a ride."

"What about Lina?" Doug asked.

"Lina! I couldn't stand another hour in that woman's company this week, and besides, I don't like owing her favours."

"Hi, guys," Peter called brightly from the living-room doorway. "Did you sell a lot of food?"

"Best day all week, better than last Saturday," Doug said. "My suppliers didn't have hardly nothing to take back. It all got sold."

"If you're so rich, big shot, how about treating us all to dinner out tonight?" Charlotte said, smiling.

"I told you, Ma," Doug said. "You got to have money

to make money, and I can't have it if I spend it right away."

"Stingy," Charlotte teased, but her eyes were admiring as she looked at her solidly built son, who had Zeke's brown eyes and broad cheekbones. Shari finished setting the table and positioned herself in the doorway beside Peter, who stood listening to the conversation.

"You'd have your own money if you'd stop smoking so much," Doug said to his mother. "And then if you invested what you saved with me, I'd give you a good return and you'd have more."

"I don't smoke," Charlotte said. "I only take a puff once in a while for my nerves."

"You promised Zeke you'd stop," Walter reminded her.

"And who says I haven't. What am I, surrounded by spies, like in Russia? My own children spying on me? And now I suppose you're just waiting to tell your daddy that I'm smoking up a storm!"

"We won't tell if you help us get a ride to the drag race Saturday night," Doug said.

At first, Charlotte objected that Doug and Walter were too young for Saturday-night drag races, but when Doug explained his scheme for selling canned drinks to the little kids there, Charlotte looked tempted, even though that was an illegal transaction by track rules. Her green eyes narrowed, and a smile twitched the corners of her lips. "How'd you get so smart, Doug? I bet you *do* wind up rich someday."

"Shari and me are going to get rich, too," Peter said,

suddenly inserting himself into the conversation. "We're going to find gold in the ravine."

The hoots of laughter from his brothers and mother wiped the brightness from his face. "Anyway, we did find something there," he said.

"What'd you find, a diamond ring?" Doug jeered.

"It was nothing," Shari threw in desperately, seeing the danger at once.

"But you said—" Peter accused her.

"Let's see what you found, for heaven's sake." Charlotte flicked her lighter open and lit a cigarette, sucking in her cheeks. She left the refrigerator and sat down at the table.

"Show it to Mama. You've got it, Shari," Peter said. He was eager to measure up to his brothers in his mother's eyes.

Cornered, Shari untied the bandanna by which she'd secured the glass bird to a loop of her jeans. The bird looked iridescent in the lamplight, the curves of its neck and wings as slippery with light as a stream of running water. She set it onto her mother's palm, holding her breath in the hope that Charlotte wouldn't see it as valuable enough to claim. Charlotte set her cigarette down in the misshapen ceramic ashtray Lina had made for her and turned the bird around and around in the pink, scoop-nailed ends of her fingers. "It's pretty," she announced. "It could be crystal. I seen something like it in the mall in the fancy shop."

"Is it a treasure?" Peter asked hopefully.

"Where'd you kids find it?" Charlotte wanted

to know.

"In the stream, down from where the bridge crosses," Shari said.

"Finders keepers," Peter thought to say.

"You took your little brother down that steep gorge? Don't you have more sense than to take him to such a dangerous place?" Charlotte demanded.

"It's not dangerous," Shari said.

"And what are you going to do when he falls and breaks his neck? Tell me how sorry you are then?"

"I won't let him fall."

"You just better not.... I can't believe you found this just laying there in the stream," Charlotte said.

"Right where the robbers' car is wrecked," Peter assured her.

"But it wasn't in the car. It was in the stream," Shari qualified.

"So that's it," Charlotte said. "It was part of what those boys stole from that woman that lives alone on the mountain—what's her name again? The one that don't come from around here."

Shari shrugged for an answer. Her fingers gripped the back of a chair while her eyes held on to the swan pincered between Charlotte's shell-tipped fingers.

"Her name's Mrs. Wallace," Walter said. Walter remembered everything. He could recite the plots of dozens of science fiction books and recall all the characters' names.

"The newspaper said a lot of stuff they took from her had only sentimental value. She collected things from where she'd lived all over the world," Charlotte mused. "It might be worth something to her to get this back."

"Please," Shari said, "can I have my bird now?"

"It's not yours," Charlotte snapped. "Don't you know you can't keep what's not yours?"

"But I found it."

"Didn't you hear what I just explained to you, dummy? ... Listen, you go up there tomorrow, and here's what you do. You don't let on you found it. Just describe it and ask if it's hers and if she'd pay a reward to get it back. Say you could get it for her if there was a reward." Charlotte studied Shari, who stood helplessly gripping the chair back. "Are you paying attention to me?"

"Please, Mother," Shari whispered. "Let me keep it."

"What would Zeke say if he heard you wanted to keep something that's not even yours? I'm ashamed of you."

"It's not stealing if you find something and keep it," Shari dared to argue.

"It is if you know who the owner is," Charlotte said. "Listen, if she gives you a reward, you can keep half. Ask her for five dollars. Tell her you'll get it back to her for five. Okay?"

Shari turned her back on her mother in despair. If Zeke were home—but he wasn't. There was no one to whom Shari could appeal.

"What's the matter with you?" Charlotte asked irritably. "You're such a weird kid. I'm offering you half. Isn't that fair enough?"

It struck Shari that Charlotte would never expect Doug

and Walter to give her half of anything they found, so why expect it of Shari? But that hardly mattered. Shari was used to Charlotte's unfairness. It was having to give up the bird that hurt. "May I have it in my room just for tonight?" she asked, avoiding her mother's eyes.

"Why not?" Charlotte was agreeable now that she'd won. "Listen, if she won't pay any reward, you just keep the thing as far as I'm concerned."

"But you said it's hers."

"So what? Didn't you find it? You didn't *take* it, did you?"

Charlotte's sudden shift in judgment was too abrupt for Shari to follow—another case where Charlotte set the rules to suit herself. Full of energy and cheerful now, she began pulling food out of the refrigerator saying, "I think I got some meat here somewhere if it hasn't gone bad yet. Get me the tomatoes and marrow, Walter. Come on, Shari. Help me get this supper started."

After the dishes were done, Shari left her family sprawled in the living room watching television and took the bird up the uncarpeted stairs to her room. No gleam in it now. Charlotte's touch must have dulled it. The hand that had opened the bedroom window last summer had long pointed fingernails. Shari boxed the knowledge away fast along with all the other hidden items in the attic of her mind. It was dangerous to know, dangerous because knowing might loose the anger, and what could Shari do with it then? All the pinches and slaps, all the razor-blade words, all the unfairnesses had to be boxed and forgotten for safety's sake.

She could have told her seventh-grade English teacher that that was where her childhood had gone. It was locked away so that Shari couldn't remember any experiences to write in the journal she had been required to keep for class.

"Such an easy assignment, Shari. Just to write about something you remember from when you were little. *Everybody* has some memories," the teacher had said.

"But I don't," Shari had answered truthfully.

On the next report card, the teacher had written under "comments" in the behaviour section, "Shari's shyness makes her appear less socially mature than other girls her age. She needs to learn to relate to others better and to express herself more openly both orally and in writing."

"What kind of garbage is this?" Charlotte had said when she saw the report card. Instead of being furious with Shari, Charlotte had called the teacher and asked, "What do you mean, not socially mature? Shari don't need to go around acting like a sixteen-year-old and wind up pregnant like some other girls her age I could name. There's nothing wrong with her. Why shouldn't she keep to herself instead of associating with the trash you got in that school?"

Shari couldn't remember another time that Charlotte had stood up for her, and she couldn't fathom why Charlotte had chosen to this time, but then her mother's moods had always been unpredictable.

Her small, bare room sloped to the shape of the roof on the side where her battered dressing table stood. A bed fitted below the window on the second wall. Zeke had put a clothes pole and shelves along the third wall for her belongings. Shari tacked the poster Peter had given her at the narrow end of the room where she could lie in bed and look at it. It was her favourite birthday present, she had told Peter. Last year her favourite present had been the live green-and-yellow parakeet Zeke had brought home to her. She still had the cage. It stood empty on the shelf above her winter boots and next to the toy record player that didn't work, and the broken doll with the voluminous lace skirt that Zeke had brought her years ago from one of his long-distance hauls. She had never much liked dolls, but anything Zeke gave her held the warmth of his affection for her, and so she treasured all his presents.

She sat on her bed, leaning against the window frame. Moonlight fell on the crystal bird in her hands. Tomorrow she had to return it to the lady who owned it—Mrs. Wallace. "It doesn't matter," Shari whispered, trying to convince herself. "It doesn't matter that it isn't mine."

Long ago she had learned to shield herself against pain when her mother hit her, but the non-physical hurts were hardest to deny. "It doesn't matter," she repeated, sealing off her heart. To feel nothing was better, to remove herself so that the body that was there didn't hold her anymore. Then after a while the danger would go away, and if she was reminded of the hurt, it would be just another item to box away.

The bird glistened in the moonlight. It nestled in the palm of her hand like a comforting charm that promised good fortune. The night air rustled with the sounds of wind-stroked leaves and the rasping hum of insects. A birdcall curled musically through the darkness.

She slept and dreamed that she was drifting through her bedroom window, holding the crystal bird, whose outstretched wings were beating in long slow strokes against the night air. She felt herself rising through the fingering leaves of her tree until the bird passed the topmost twigs and she could see the stars far and away above her. Then she climbed onto the bird's back. It had grown to an enormous size, and its wings shimmered with moonlight.

The cool wind swished past as the crystal bird sailed through the night, more magnificent than the hawks whose proud domination of the sky she had envied as they hovered over the valley. Jewel clusters beneath her were the lights of houses, and the twin diamonds and rubies strung sparsely in a straight line were the head- and tail-lights of the cars passing on the highway below.

Joy fluttered inside her. She was flying, flying, flying as she had always dreamed, where no earthly thing could touch her, free of all bounds. If she could have, she would have sailed through the blackness of space through aeons of time to reach the constellations of stars overhead, so powerful did she feel as she swooped through the night, skimming the mountaintops, soaring gloriously above them. Around and up and down and around again in great swirls of motion, like the tilt-a-whirl Zeke had taken them on at the county fair.

She awoke the next morning with the exhilaration of her passage still fresh, feeling renewed.

Three

"*Come on, kids*," Charlotte yelled. "Get down here for breakfast. I got a surprise for you today."

Shari sat up in bed wondering what could have caused the happy carolling of her mother's voice. Could Zeke have called to say he was coming home sooner than they expected? Or was the surprise just an invitation from BeeJay? Last month BeeJay took the whole family to the pets' corner at the shopping mall, and she had even bought an entrance ticket for Peter. Charlotte had gone inside with him while the rest of them watched the animals through the chain-link fence. Nice, but not as good as having Zeke come home.

Shari picked up the crystal bird and looked at it. Today she had to return it to Mrs. Wallace, unless something lucky happened. If Zeke was coming home, Charlotte might just forget the bird. Or Zeke might say Shari didn't have to return it. Shari wondered if he'd think she had to just because she knew who the real owner was. Probably he would say she should. That was the honest thing to do.

Shari put on yesterday's cut-off jeans and a tee shirt Walter had outgrown. It had a cartoon of Roadrunner on it and was getting nubbly, but had no holes yet. She brushed her hair, undisturbed by the lack of a mirror in her room. Charlotte had offered to get her one for her birthday last year, but Shari had asked for money to spend on her parakeet instead. "That's the last pet we're having in this house!" Charlotte had said after Chirpy flew away. She'd been angry at Shari for mooning by her open window all week in the hope that he'd return.

"I got enough human animals to take care of around here," Charlotte had complained to Zeke. "No more birds, or dogs either."

Walter had protested that it wasn't his fault that his mixed-breed Alsatian had bitten Peter, and he couldn't help it that the dog got killed chasing a car down the highway or that Shari's bird flew away.

"No more pets," Charlotte had repeated, and Zeke took her side as usual.

"After all," he told Walter, "I'm gone most of the time, and your mother's stuck with all the headaches. You got to understand, Walt; she's got more than she can handle as it is."

Zeke had a lot of sympathy for his wife. "Don't take what your mother says too hard," he'd told Shari once when he heard Charlotte picking on her. "She don't mean half what she says. It's her nerves, that's all."

Charlotte was bouncing about energetically as Shari entered the kitchen. "So what if you don't open your stand one day," she was saying to a sour-faced Doug as she fixed his eggs at the stove. "How often do we get an invitation to go swimming anyway? You're only twelve years old, kid. Live a little."

Doug's hammer-ended chin set stubbornly in his broad face, but he said nothing.

"*I* want to go, Ma," Walter said through a bite of hamburger roll oozing jam. "But my cut-offs are too full of holes to swim in."

"Well, find something else to wear," Charlotte said. "I'm not sewing up those crummy cut-offs again."

"Then I'm not going." Walter folded his arms across his chest and shoved himself back from the table as if to remove himself from the family.

"I can't believe you kids!" Charlotte said. "BeeJay invites us all to the lake with her and you sit there and give me a hard time about it. Listen, for all I care, you can all stay home and I'll go without you."

"What about me?" Peter demanded. "I haven't been swimming all summer."

"I'd like to go," Shari said quietly.

"Well, hurry up and get ready then," Charlotte said. "BeeJay'll be here in a few minutes, and we got to fix some lunch to take."

"I can't go without my cut-offs," Walter said. Lately he'd become self-conscious about his bulky body. He insisted on keeping his hair long enough to cover his open-hinge ears and would only wear particular items of clothing that he thought suited him.

"You could wear my shorts," Shari offered. "They'd fit you, and I'll wear my old shorts to swim in."

"I'm not wearing girl's pants." Walter looked horrified.

"They were Doug's originally," Shari pointed out

37

to him.

"We'll buy drinks at the lake," Charlotte muttered to herself as she stuffed bread and baloney and mustard and peanut butter and jam, along with a knife for spreading and cutting, into the white Styrofoam cooler.

"My suppliers will get mad if I'm not there when they deliver the stuff I'm supposed to sell for them," Doug said.

"No, they won't. Just leave a sign. You can tell them your mother made you go. You're only a kid. What can they expect?" Charlotte said.

Abandoning the toast she had made for herself, Shari ran upstairs to change her clothes and bring her cut-offs down to Walter. She liked the lake, enjoyed basking in the sun, listening to waves slap hollow sounds from the oil drums that buoyed up the raft on which she lay. When she got back to the kitchen, Walter took the cut-offs without a word and went into the bathroom. Doug was on the phone talking to the lady who grew the tomatoes he sold.

"Don't tell anyone I'm wearing your cut-offs," Walter said to Shari when he came out.

She remembered the time Zeke had caught Walter reading a book as he sat beside Doug, who had the TV going at top volume. "Walter, did you learn how to read while riding your bike yet?" Zeke had joked. "Figure out how to read in the dark?" Walter had been so embarrassed he'd stuffed his book behind the cushions in the sofa and hadn't read another thing for a day. He couldn't take teasing, but Shari wished she could escape into books the way he could. When his eyes hunted back and forth across a page, he was oblivious of everything else. He read at night too, in the unfinished attic room space he shared with Doug and Peter, when everyone in the house besides her was asleep.

"What do you find in all those books?" she'd asked him, but he had no words to tell her. Like her, he took in a lot but let out little.

BeeJay honked the horn of her little red car with the black racing stripes.

"Lock the back door," Charlotte yelled and ran outside with the picnic box.

Peter slipped his hand into Shari's. "I don't need my water wings this year. I'm going to really swim."

"Wait," Shari said, remembering. "I'll get the inner tube." She ran to the carport where she'd last seen the tube, found it under the tangled garden hose and dashed to BeeJay's car with it. The tube would be fun for all of them.

Peter was fidgeting outside the car. Everybody else was already in it. As soon as Shari saw BeeJay's clumsy black Labrador retriever on the back seat between Doug and Walter, she understood.

"All right, you can sit up front with me if you're such a little scaredy cat," Charlotte was saying to Peter.

"I'm not getting in no car with that dog," Peter whined.

His fear was so huge Shari could almost see it. Ever since he'd been bitten by Walter's Alsatian, he'd been afraid of big dogs. He would need to be protected from the restless BoBo. The dog's head hung over the front seat, red tongue flopping while he nudged first BeeJay and then Charlotte for attention.

"All right then, Peter," Charlotte said ominously. "You can just stay home." Tears spilled from Peter's eyes, but he didn't budge. "Shari, you stay with him," Charlotte said. "We don't need to be crowded in this car for a kid who don't even appreciate going."

"That's the ticket, Charlotte," BeeJay said. "No spoiled brats on this trip." BeeJay revved the engine, grinning her rubber-mouthed grin.

Charlotte lifted tumbling locks from the back of her neck as if she were already getting hot and uncomfortable. "Listen, Shari, you can fix a can of tuna fish or something for lunch, and don't forget to see that lady like I told you."

Shari flinched. From treat to tribulation faster than the eye could follow. It had happened before, but that didn't relieve her disappointment now. The car left dust clouds on the road behind it. Peter was still crying bitterly when the dust had settled.

"Come on, Petey," Shari said, letting her anger go to concentrate on his misery. "We'll have a good time in the woods by ourselves."

"But I wanted to go to the lake."

"Me too, but we can't; so we won't fuss about it. Let's try and have fun anyway."

Her resolve was only shaken when they tried to get into the house and found it was locked front and back. Charlotte had the key with her. Shari's own key was upstairs on her dressing table.

"How're we going to eat?" Peter asked. Alarm dried up his tears. Not to eat for a day was worse for him than missing out on a swim.

"Don't worry. Mabel will let us have some doughnuts or something, and we can pay her tomorrow. You can't be hungry anyway. You just had breakfast. Let's go dig for gold again. Then we can sneak up on Mrs. Wallace's house and spy on her to see if she's nice."

"Why do you care if she's nice?" Peter asked.

"I'm not going to let her have the bird back unless she's nice."

"Mama will get mad at you if you don't."

"We'll see," Shari said, glad that she'd managed to distract him from his disappointment. "Come on. It's a long way up the mountain to her house."

He looked down the road longingly, but BeeJay's car had gone. Finally he sighed and even dredged up a smile for her as he said, "Okay. Let's go."

"You really are growing up, Peter," Shari said in praise of his quick adjustment.

They descended into the ravine and crossed the rapids, but before stopping to pan for gold, Peter suggested they do their spying on Mrs. Wallace first. "If she's nice, maybe she'll give us something to eat."

Shari laughed. "What kind of spies get invited in for a snack, Pete? She's not supposed to know we're spying on her."

"We'll see," Peter said in an echo of her own voice.

To get to Mrs. Wallace's, they had to climb the far wall of the ravine to reach a side road up the mountain. A projecting ledge of rock made a lip along the top edge of this wall of the ravine. Peter balked when they got to it. "I'm not climbing over that," he said. "No way." He looked nervously over his shoulder at the gravelly descent to the stream, which seemed forever below them.

"It's not as bad as it looks," Shari said. "I'll go first and find the toeholds."

"No," Peter said. "I can't do it. I'll fall."

"Relax," she said. "Soon as I'm up, I'll lower something you can hold on to. I didn't ever let you fall, did I?"

She left him clinging to a wedge of rock and twisted shrub and pulled herself from bare toehold to bare toehold, up and over the ledge, grasping exposed tree roots where she could. At the top, she lay belly down with her head hanging over the edge to tell him, "See, it's not so hard. I'll get something to lower to you so you can hold on as you climb up."

"I can't, Shari," he whined. "I'm scared."

"Want me to come back down and you can hold on to me as you come up?"

"I'm not good at climbing."

"Sure you are. Your only problem is your muscles aren't strong enough yet, but when you're older, you'll be as good a climber as me."

"No, I won't. I'm never going to be good at nothing. I wish I never got born into our family."

"You don't want me for a sister any more?"

He considered that, looking troubled as he made up his mind. Finally he took a deep breath and said, "You better help me up there so I don't fall." Then he looked down fearfully to where the stream rushed over rocks and branches below them.

"Be right back," Shari said and hurried to find a strong, thin tree limb that she could reach down to him. Fortunately, she didn't have to go far. This back road was so untravelled that broken tree branches from last winter's storms still lay on its shoulders. Peter took the end of the branch she thrust towards him in both hands and clung for all he was worth as she hauled him up, but he did help by using his feet for climbing when she asked him to. She would not have been strong enough to pull him up otherwise.

"There," she said jubilantly, when they were resting side by side on the top of the rock. "I told you it wasn't so hard."

"I did it," he said proudly.

She smiled and hugged him and agreed, "Yes, you did. Didn't I tell you you're getting to be a big boy?"

He hugged her back cozily, the way he always had, and she was glad he didn't feel too grown up for hugging.

They walked up the shady side of the tarmacked mountain road until they came to an unmade road marked private. Mrs. Wallace's name was on a post beside it. Two tyre-track ruts with a weed-grown hump between them led up steeply through overgrown woods and fields of blackberry and mullein and goldenrod.

"What if she sees us?" Peter asked.

"We'll tell her we're looking for something," Shari said, and tried to think of what. She wasn't good at white lies. She hated talking to adults. Shyness made her voice disappear, and she often blurted out things that didn't sound right before dashing off in embarrassment.

"We could just tell her we got lost," Peter suggested.

"We could," Shari said, squeezing his hand gratefully.

"I can talk to her," Peter offered. "I like to talk to people."

"You're good at it," Shari agreed, "better than me." She took a deep breath of spicy juniper and scented field flowers and admired the clump of tousled birches. A chipmunk skittered past them to the safety of a rock pile. Its golden brown body wore a flag of black and white stripes. "Everything's so pretty in the woods," Shari said.

"Are we almost there?" Peter asked. The woods had never much interested him.

"Must be." Shari hoped so for his sake.

As they rounded the last curve in the road, the house appeared. It was a sturdy wooden cottage with a steeply pitched roof like a witch's hat. They recognized Mrs. Wallace's pick-up truck in front of the open garage, which was built into the hillside below the house. The house seemed set to view the ranges of mountain peaks that piled up in the distance, each paler and farther off than the peaks before it, wave upon wave of mountain peaks into the hazy horizon.

Shari tugged urgently at Peter's hand. They had to get out of sight in case someone was watching them. She drew him off the road, and they squatted behind a clump of weeds. A screen door snapped shut. There stood Mrs. Wallace. Shari had seen her passing by in her truck and once in Mabel's store. She was a stumpy-looking lady with a neat cap of short white hair framing a round, bright face with clear grey eyes that seemed to see great distances. She didn't look that old, Shari thought. Shari liked the straight, capable look the woman had, a no-nonsense look emphasized by the plain clothes Mrs. Wallace wore—jeans and a loose plaid shirt with rolled-up sleeves. But how people looked didn't always tell how they were inside. Charlotte was pretty, and BeeJay's rubbery mouth gave a humorous impression, but neither of them could be trusted.

At first, it seemed the swallows darting from their mud nests along the eaves of Mrs. Wallace's roof and swooping down over her head might be trying to protect their territory. Then Shari realized from the playful way they looped around the front lawn and wheeled back to Mrs. Wallace on the porch again, like dancers skimming the air, that they were greeting a friend. Mrs. Wallace proceeded briskly down the steps to the garage under her house and disappeared from view.

"Is she going away?" Peter whispered.

"I don't know."

"Can you tell anything yet?"

"Not yet. Let's move farther along so we can see the side and back yard." She let Peter lead the way. He crawled under the trailing branches of a spruce, and Shari followed into the evergreen cave.

Mrs. Wallace had only lived up here for three or four years, but had owned this property for much longer. She and her husband had built her house before he died. Shari knew that and also that Mabel was Mrs. Wallace's friend,

45

her only friend in town because Mrs. Wallace wasn't a churchgoer and didn't associate much with anybody else. "Probably thinks she's too good for us country folk," Charlotte said when Lina had wondered aloud why Mrs. Wallace didn't attend church. Neither of Shari's parents were churchgoers either.

"She likes to keep to herself," Lina had said, "but she acts normal enough, she's not crazy or nothing, I mean."

When Mrs. Wallace emerged from the garage with a forty-pound bag of birdseed in a wheelbarrow, Shari's heart beat faster. Mrs. Wallace began filling bird feeders. Two wee grey-crested birds with pale, round breasts promptly arrived to feast at the window-shelf feeder, and a noisy blue jay chased a trio of black-capped chickadees who were doing gymnastics about the large feeder on a post.

"Scat, you bully," Mrs. Wallace told the blue jay. It ignored the scolding but kept an eye cocked at her as it gobbled up sunflower seeds. "Think just because you're handsome that I'd invite the likes of you to dinner?" Mrs. Wallace said to the jay. "I don't like your manners." She waved a branch at the jay, which removed itself to a nearby tree.

"Who's she talking to?" Peter whispered.

"She doesn't like blue jays. I don't either," Shari said. "They're mean to other birds."

Mrs. Wallace turned the corner of her house, and suddenly Shari heard a rush of feathers and Mrs. Wallace's voice, soothing now. "Seems you're feeling better, fellow. And you're certainly looking proud this morning.

Shall we see what you can do on your own? Shall we try that wing out on the wind today?"

"Come on," Peter whispered, with his hand cupped to Shari's ear. He walked boldly into the open and ducked back into the woods, hiding where the far corner of the house was visible. Hesitantly, Shari followed his lead. She crouched next to him, but all she could see was a caterpillar eating its way through a leaf in front of her nose.

"She's got a big bird in a cage," Peter whispered and moved aside so that Shari could trade places with him.

Hawk! Shari thought, and her heart squeezed with excitement as she saw the large cage made out of an old rabbit hutch, and the angular-headed bird with the curved beak. It was not much bigger than a robin, but by its beautiful speckled breast and rusty-coloured back and tail, she knew it was a sparrow hawk. Mrs. Wallace was reaching into the cage with a leather gardening glove on her hand. She tossed in something grasshopper sized that the hawk struck at and swallowed. It lifted its wings slightly as it moved on its board perch. The perch was fixed to a broom handle stuck through the cage wires with the ragged-edged broom still attached. The sparrow hawk kept dipping its tail as if to keep its balance, and Mrs. Wallace continued to toss the contents of a plastic bag, piece by piece, into its cage.

"That should hold you for a while," Mrs. Wallace said, and then asked the bird: "Well, what do you say? Is today the day? You can fly back for a handout tomorrow if you need to." She stood aside, leaving the cage door open. The hawk looked around, head tensed. It jumped to the doorway and without hesitation leaped into the air with pointed wings stretched wide and laser eyes intent on freedom. A few flaps of its wings and the hawk had crossed the yard and disappeared into the woods where they dropped away down the mountainside.

Mrs. Wallace waited as if she expected more. She drew off her glove and chewed at the edge of her thumb. Peter stirred restlessly and slapped at a mosquito. A minute passed slowly before anything happened.

"Look," Shari whispered as the hawk flew up out of the woods. Rising swiftly, it gained height until it no longer needed to beat down on the air but could float on the currents gracefully, a black silhouette the shape of a giant swallow against the high blue heavens. It circled overhead higher and higher until at last it was out of sight.

"She set him free," Shari whispered reverently. "She fixed him and set him free."

"He won't die in the woods like Chirpy, will he?" Peter asked.

"Not him. He's a hawk, Peter."

"Well, do you think she's nice then?"

"Yes."

"So do you want me to talk to her now?"

"No need."

"Why not?" He began scratching his mosquito bites. She knew his stomach had to be close to empty and considered heading down to Mabel's store and begging lunch.

"Come on," Shari murmured. "We have to sneak out of here without letting her see us."

"But you didn't ask her about the reward."

"I'm not going to."

"You're going to keep the bird?"

"No. I'll leave it by her front door tomorrow morning before she gets up."

"Then how will she know who to give the reward to?"

"I don't want any reward for finding her swan." Shari couldn't explain it better than that, even though Peter looked confused and kept asking her why not.

"Mama will kill you," he warned.

"I don't care. Anyway, maybe Zeke will get home tomorrow, and he won't let her."

As they left, Shari glanced back and saw Mrs. Wallace still standing with fingers pressed into the small of her arched back as she stared at the Presidential Range, which rose in still grey waves beyond the green crests of the nearby mountains. How wonderful, Shari thought, to find a person who liked the same things she did. She hadn't known anyone like herself existed in the world. It was right that the crystal bird should belong to Mrs. Wallace, and if Shari was lucky enough to see her face when she opened her front door and found it on her doorstep, that would be reward enough.

Four

"*Don't think* just because Zeke's coming home that you're getting away with it," Charlotte had warned when she found out what Shari had done with the crystal bird. "I'll teach you you can't do just like you please. Think you can act like what I tell you don't matter? You just wait, Shari Ape Face."

The vague threat was more frightening than the quick slap or pinch, the violent yank on a handful of Shari's long hair. It raised grey images of past punishments—the classmate's birthday party Shari had been kept from attending at the last minute, the doll she had been forced to share with her younger brothers, who ruined it, the garage-sale dress Charlotte had bought two sizes too big and insisted Shari wear on the first day of school last year, and furthest back, before Peter was born, a day spent tied to the leg of a bed while rain drummed on the roof of the empty house.

Shari ventured up from the basement where Charlotte had sent her to sort and fold the washing. The living room looked unfamiliar with everything picked up. Uncluttered by discarded clothes and fizzy drinks cans and books and toys, it looked bare. This morning Charlotte had given them all cleaning-up assignments and instructed. "Now don't start messing up the place before your father gets home. Be careful you don't miss the toilet bowl, and leave the clean towels alone until tomorrow."

Charlotte's hair was done in a mass of curls, like a young girl's, and she wore a new scoop-necked pink stretch top and lipstick that matched. She kept dashing between the kitchen, where she had an apple pie baking for Zeke's belated birthday celebration, and the front window, where she and Peter were keeping watch.

On Zeke's first day home, Charlotte's game was to treat him like a guest. It was a game they all liked to play, fun until the inevitable moment when Charlotte started telling Zeke all the things "his" kids had done wrong and all the appliances that had failed and the chores that needed doing. Zeke would wince at her change in tone and try to hold her off a while longer. "Now, Charl, I'll take care of it," he would say. "Just relax. I'll get to it eventually." He'd handle the discipline, meting out fair judgments and moderate punishments, and until he left again, the soothing sound of saw and hammer and axe would lull Charlotte. She would relax and be easygoing, even playful, with Zeke. Then the call would come for him to pick up a load of apples or lumber or light fixtures for delivery in Dubuque or Atlanta or Chicago where still other goods awaited shipment back and forth on the highways across America. Sometimes he was gone for only a few days, but often it was weeks.

Shari couldn't remember how it had been when Zeke worked for a meat-packing company in Rutland and came home every night. She had been Peter's age then. When Charlotte spoke of those years with longing, Zeke would say to her, "Come on; get off it, sweetheart. You know we fought all the time. You were always on my back."

"No, I wasn't. How can you say such a thing? I don't nag," Charlotte would protest.

"Don't nag?" Zeke would laugh. "I bet you'd take first prize in a nagging contest anywhere in the U.S.A." He'd grin when she exploded and cajole her with, "Never mind. You're still my sweet girl. It's okay. I know you got to complain to someone and it might as well be me. All's I'm saying is, we're better off the way things are. And the money's better too, isn't it?"

"Yes," she would agree reluctantly to that, and the discussion would end until the next time.

"He's here!" Peter shrilled. He leaped from his perch on the back of the chair to run to the front door.

Excitement bubbled in the air, and everybody smiled, including Walter and Doug, who had been at their stand and were now hanging out the windows of Zeke's rig. The big cab looked misshapen with its over-sized wheels and no trailer behind it. Zeke blew his sonorous horn, announcing his arrival far and wide in the valley. He parked the cab and jumped from it, arms out to receive Charlotte in a swinging hug and a long kiss. Peter hopped impatiently onto his father's broad back, while Zeke swayed Charlotte back and forth in his arms as if he couldn't bear to let go of her. She looked small and girlish against his burly form.

"Glad to see me, honey? Glad to see your old man?" Zeke asked her, grinning.

"You big old bear. You could've shaved." But he never shaved until the morning after he arrived. His ritual was to grow his beard and moustache all the while he was gone and shave it off when he got home.

Now Zeke was dangling Peter from his arm, letting him hang like a side of beef being weighed on a butcher's scale. "You're getting there, fella. Going to be as big as your brothers any day now."

"What'd you bring me?" Peter asked. "Something to eat?" He preferred eating presents, the pecans from Georgia, dates and figs from California and Arizona, fruitcakes from the South. Zeke always brought each of them something. Last time he'd given them geodes from the desert, round stone balls that might have interesting crystals inside or might not. Shari still had hers intact in her room. She couldn't bear to split the grey shell apart in case nothing at all was inside. Once, Zeke had brought her a beaded Indian vest made of deerskin, a marvellous present that made her wonder if her father knew she'd like to have been an Indian. She hadn't got around to asking him before Charlotte lent the vest to an acquaintance's daughter to use in a school play. Shari hadn't got it back, even though she'd forced herself past her shyness to ask the girl to return it.

"You're going to mess up my new outfit," Charlotte squealed as Zeke gave her another squeeze.

"Come inside and I'll mess you up some more where the neighbours can't see," Zeke said. And then he remembered Shari. "Where's my little girl? Where's my littlest sweetheart?"

Shari rushed from the doorway, reaching up her arms for his rough hug and kiss. "I'm so glad you're home, Daddy," she said huskily.

"Hey, Dad," Doug said, as they trooped after Zeke into the living room. "There's going to be a carnival this weekend. Could you take us?"

"We'll see. First I got to sleep for about a week to make up for all the time I lost on the road."

"Can I go to the carnival too, Daddy, please? Can I go too?" Peter begged.

"How long will you be home this time?" Charlotte asked him anxiously, and before he had a chance to answer, "You didn't notice my new hair style. Do you like it?"

"It's beautiful, Charl. You're beautiful. You get prettier instead of older."

She giggled and leaned against him, asking, "Glad to see me, honey? Glad to see me after so long on the road?"

"Glad's not the half of it," he told her and caught Peter in a headlock, pretending not to notice as Pete squawked to be let loose.

"Well," Zeke said to Charlotte, "shall I wash up first, or are you going to offer me a beer?"

"I'm going to invite you into the kitchen. We got a surprise for you," she said. She took his arm possessively, tucking hers around his meaty one. "I hope you're hungry."

"Ain't I always?"

With his free hand, he patted Shari's back as if to acknowledge her existence as he let his wife lead him into the kitchen, where balloons were hung from the light fixture and the sweet, cinnamony aroma of apple pie filled the air. The small presents they had bought or made for him were waiting in a pile beside his plate.

"Surprise, surprise. Happy birthday," Charlotte said, echoed in a round by the children.

"Is it my birthday?" Zeke asked.

"You had it last week on the road, but we're celebrating now," Doug patiently explained.

"You know, you're right. I got a whole year older while I wasn't even looking. Imagine that!"

Without being asked, Doug got a beer for his father and opened it. "Can Walt and me have one too, Dad?"

"You kids can have a sip of mine, seeing as this is a celebration," Zeke said and sat down at his place at the table with an exaggerated sigh of satisfaction. "Lord, it is *good* to be home," he said. Immediately Peter clamoured for his father to open his presents, but Zeke wasn't to be rushed. He liked to sniff at things and shake them and guess until his family was wild with the suspense, even though they knew well enough what was inside each package. Charlotte had bought him a new anorak to replace the one he'd left at a café somewhere. Walter and Doug had chipped in for ammunition for his deer-hunting rifle. Peter had bought a cigar, even though Zeke didn't smoke. Shari's gift was chocolate fudge she'd made herself.

"Sweets from my little girl," Zeke said. "What could

be better?"

"You know what your sweet little girl went and did?" Charlotte asked irritably, breaking her truce day for the first time ever. They hadn't finished the birthday celebration; they hadn't even got to her apple pie. "You know what she did?" Charlotte repeated, without looking at Shari who was quivering at this unexpected outbreak of her mother's fury.

"Do you really want to tell me now?" Zeke asked with a flatness that revealed his lack of enthusiasm for hearing what Shari had done.

"Well, it'll keep you from acting like a fool being nice to this stuck-up kid who thinks she's too good to pick up easy money when she gets the chance. Thinks we're rich or something."

"She is rich," Zeke said. "She's got everything she needs including a loving family, don't she?"

"A little extra money never hurts," Charlotte said. "Anyway, why are you defending her right off before you hear what happened?"

"And why are you starting in before I've had a chance to relax and get acquainted with my family again. Or do you only want me home to hear your complaints?"

His anger deflated Charlotte instantly. She seemed to shrink as she stood at the stove, and her voice was thin as she asked him, "You want your steak well done like usual?"

Now it was his turn to gear down. "Let's not fight, Charl," he begged. "Let's just—"

She flashed her eyes at him. "Always what *you* need.

Think it's so easy being alone here with these kids night and day for weeks on end? Think I got it so good?"

Zeke sighed and finished his beer in two gulps. "Okay," he said to his daughter. "How'd you lose us a fortune, Shari baby?"

Tonelessly she told him. "I found something, and Mama thought I could get a reward for it, but I returned it to the lady and didn't ask her for anything. Mama said I had to return it. She said it belonged to Mrs. Wallace."

"What was it?"

"Just a glass bird. It was really pretty."

"It was crystal. I saw something like it that cost a small fortune in the fancy gift shop in the mall," Charlotte added.

"And what'd Mrs. Wallace say when you gave it back to her, Shari?" Zeke asked.

Shari hung her head. "Nothing—to me. I just left it on her steps this morning and hid in the woods until she came outside."

"Why'd you wait?"

"To see her face. She looked happy, Daddy. And I heard her say, 'Oh, my, how on earth did this get back here?'"

"But you were too shy to talk to her."

Shari shrugged and didn't correct him. It was true being shy had been part of it. The rest was a sense that it would taint the charm of the bird to demand money for returning it to its rightful owner. She wished she had the words to make Zeke understand.

"Shy my eye," Charlotte said. "She was just out to

spite me. She just refuses no matter what I ask her. You think she's so sweet, but you don't see what she's like when you're not around."

"I do everything you tell me," Shari was stung into protesting. "I do everything you say."

"All right, now," Zeke said. "If this is how it's going to go, I'm calling the dispatch office and getting the next load out of here. No way am I going to tolerate all this scrapping."

"Then why don't you tell that kid to shut her face?" Charlotte yelled, no longer pretty now that she was bulging red with outrage. "Whose side are you on, mine or the kids? You come home after drinking beer all around the country with your road buddies and won't even back me up. You leave me to deal with these kids who are always into something and won't listen. Think it's fun, living here alone in this rat-hole town?"

The homecoming celebration had ended so abruptly that they never got to eat the apple pie. Zeke concentrated on calming Charlotte down, being extra attentive to get her back into a good mood. He told her she was his darling, and, of course, he understood how hard she had it with him gone all the time, and she was a wonderful, brave woman, and didn't she want to see the trinket he'd brought her? Wouldn't she come upstairs with him? The kids could do the dishes. He'd visit with them tomorrow.

Neither parent had come downstairs again. Doug fell asleep in front of the television set. Walter settled forth into a book, his eyes riding steadily back and forth across the pages. Peter kept asking when they were going to eat the pie.

"We can't until Zeke has his piece," Shari said and finally told Peter it was time for him to go to bed. He was half-asleep and crabby as she stood him in front of the toilet and made sure he aimed at the bowl instead of the wall. Then she got him to wash his face and hands and brush his teeth before he rolled into bed in his underpants. She covered him and kissed him goodnight and went to her own bedroom.

The squeaking of bedsprings and Charlotte's low laugh came through the thin wall of Shari's bedroom. From past experience, Shari knew her parents would be all right in the morning. She wondered, as she lay in bed listening to the night sounds outside, if telling on her to Zeke had been enough punishment to satisfy Charlotte, or if more was still coming because Shari had not asked for the reward. It was hard to know with Charlotte. Little things enraged her, yet she'd overlook serious ones altogether.

Maybe after Zeke fixed Charlotte's car and before she put him to work on the septic tank that was beginning to smell in the backyard, Zeke would take them all to the lake for a swim or to the carnival Doug had mentioned. It was always better when Zeke was around. Chances were he wouldn't be angry with Shari, and if she was lucky, she'd get some stray moments alone with him.

Five

For two days Zeke worked on Charlotte's car, replacing a head gasket and correcting the engine's faulty timing, while Shari and Peter hung just back of his elbow. They brought him rags for wiping greasy engine parts and beers for quenching his thirst while he treated the car's ailments.

"Don't think I've finished with you," Charlotte had warned, but Shari didn't let the threat mar her enjoyment of Zeke's good-humoured presence, the occasional hug, the back rub with the knuckles of his greasy fingers. In a moment of mischief, when the temperature had hit the nineties and Zeke was raining perspiration even working in the shade of the trees, Shari turned the garden hose on him.

"How about me?" Peter asked promptly, and Zeke laughed as she drenched them both.

"Okay, now this time it's going to work," Zeke announced for the fifth time, after his hose shower. "Start her up, Pete."

They cheered when the engine fired and continued running. "Told you!" Zeke said jubilantly. "Just give me the tools and the time and I can fix it."

"Why don't you open a garage?" Shari said. "Then you could stay home with us all the time." She knew he had worked in a garage before he was married.

"It'd be nice, but it takes money to start something like that, and there's no guarantee I'd make enough from it to keep us in groceries even if I had the money to get started." The garage Zeke had worked in had failed to make a profit and had gone out of business long ago.

"We could be your helpers," Peter said eagerly. "We'd work cheap."

Zeke ruffled Peter's hair and said, "You and Shari sure are good helpers, but I'd better keep the job I have. There's plenty of men in this country would be glad to get my job."

"Zeke," Shari said, taking the hand he offered her as they walked to the house. "What do you have to do to be a flyer? To pilot a jet, I mean?"

"A pilot? Who'd want to do that?"

"Me."

"You?" He stopped and stared at her. "Where'd you get that idea, Shari? Who's been talking to you?"

Shari flinched from the sudden tension in his voice and pulled her hand from his, even though she couldn't remember the last time Zeke had been angry with her. "It's my own idea. I'd just like to . . . It's just what I want to be, Daddy."

For a minute he studied her. Then he relaxed and said, "Sorry, honey. I didn't mean to scare you. It's just, I knew a feller once who was a pilot. I didn't like him. . . . I guess to fly a big plane you got to take lessons, and it'd cost plenty—more than we've got. I wouldn't count on becoming a pilot if I was you. Why don't you think of something you can do closer to home?"

As they were about to enter the house, Zeke added in a low voice, "Shari, one thing—don't *ever* say anything to your mother about wanting to be a pilot. Okay?"

Shari nodded without asking questions. It was only much later that she remembered Peter had already told Charlotte about her desire to fly. She wondered about the man whom Zeke hadn't liked. Had Charlotte known him too?

At supper that night Zeke announced, "Tomorrow we go to the lake and maybe take in the carnival on the way home. Doug, you put a sign on your vegetable stand that you went fishing. No arguments. You're already the richest twelve-year-old kid in town."

Next morning when Shari came downstairs in her peppermint candy-stripe swimsuit that Zeke said made her look delicious, Charlotte said to her, "What are you dressed up for? You're not going with us."

Shari stopped short at the breakfast table. "Why not?"

"I told you I was going to teach you a lesson, didn't I?" Charlotte said. "Next time maybe you'll do what I tell you."

Shari looked over at her father who was crouched over a plate of eggs, head bent nearly to his hairy forearms. "Daddy?" she asked.

He looked at her guiltily and muttered. "This is between you and your mother, Shari. She's the one in charge when I'm on the road. If she wants to punish you for what you done, then I can't interfere."

Without a word, Shari ran back to her room and threw herself down onto her carefully made-up bed. She squeezed the pillow in anger. What had she done that was so terrible? Just because she hadn't asked for a five-dollar reward, Charlotte had deprived her of the summer's best treat. That was so mean, so unfair and rotten—mean! Shari was still shaking with frustration when she heard the car engine's coughing become a steady growl.

When they had gone, the anger whooshed out of her. Zeke had left her behind. She lay listlessly while birds chatted back and forth in the tree outside her window and the silence of the empty house gathered around her. After a while, she took a deep breath and got up. Senseless to lie around indoors on a summer day. Besides, for all she knew, they might have left a message for her.

She went downstairs. Nothing in the kitchen; nothing in the bare yard except Peter's plastic pool, dirty with leaves and twigs and gravel in the few inches of leftover water in the bottom. Peter, at least, should have come to tell her he was sorry she wasn't going with them. He'd gone off without a thought for her. No loyalty in him, either. Of course, he was only six. As for Zeke, she knew that he had to appease Charlotte. Just as well he had. Times past when he'd interfered on Shari's behalf, Charlotte had made her pay double when he wasn't around. Certainly Shari couldn't expect anything from Doug and Walter. Their concern was for each other. They had never cared much about her.

"Don't think," Shari ordered herself out loud. She

would not go around feeling wronged. Stupid to make herself feel worse instead of better. The woods were still there for her. Without Peter to hold her back, she could climb and explore new places. She could make the day good for herself instead of lying around and suffering. All of a sudden, a pang of hunger reminded her that she hadn't had breakfast. The first thing to do was to eat.

For safety's sake, and because she hated the sound of gunshots, Shari didn't go far into the woods during the autumn hunting season. The rest of the year she rarely saw another person during her solitary explorations. It startled her, therefore, to see a stumpy figure in jeans and a loose shirt high up on the mountain, far from any path. Shari hid behind a tree to see without being seen. Hard to tell whether the figure studying the sky through binoculars was male or female, but the cap of white hair gave her away. What was Mrs. Wallace doing climbing around up here, Shari wondered. Did Mrs. Wallace also know the ledge Shari called Eagle's Perch?

She was used to wondering about things that her shyness kept her from investigating, and she would have slipped past unobserved if Mrs. Wallace hadn't gasped, "There he is."

As Mrs. Wallace lifted the binoculars to her eyes again, Shari stepped away from the tree so she could see out into the valley. Sure enough, it was the eagle. He had his nest in a bare-armed tree that commanded the valley and seemed to grow out from the rock ledge. Now he was resting on the wind high overhead, circling on magnificent outstretched wings. Shari watched in awe. She had looked him up in the bird book in the reference section of the library; so she knew by his size and the broad, flat, feather-fingered wings that he was a bald eagle and not a large hawk. Her impulse was to share her knowledge with Mrs. Wallace.

Mrs. Wallace raised a camera hanging from a leather strap around her neck and said aloud, "Light's wrong, darn it." She let go of both binoculars and camera to simply watch.

It was the moment for Shari to leave, but she waited until Mrs. Wallace turned and discovered her. "Good heavens!" Mrs. Wallace said. "For an instant I thought you were an Indian spirit returning to your old hunting territory. What are you doing up here, child?"

"Climbing."

"All by yourself?"

"Yes."

"Well, I'm glad to know I'm not the only one crazy enough to go wandering around mountains alone. Have you seen the eagle?"

"Yes . . . I know where he nests."

"You do?" Mrs. Wallace looked genuinely impressed. "Would you believe that's what I climbed all the way up here to find? His nest. I thought it would interest my granddaughters if I photographed it for them. Of course, I'd like a picture of that big handsome bird in the flesh, or should I say feather, as well. I don't suppose you could call him down and get him to pose for me?"

Shari smiled. "No, but I could show you where the

nest is."

"Would you? Is it within reach of an overweight, not so agile older party like me?"

Shari considered. "You could get close enough to take a picture."

"Lead on," Mrs. Wallace said. "What shall I call you?"

"I'm Shari."

"That's a pretty name. I'm Eve Wallace."

"I know."

"You do?"

Shari nodded, too embarrassed to confess her secret observation of Mrs. Wallace at her house.

"I keep forgetting that all the local people seem to know me even when I don't know them. It's an interesting phenomenon for someone like me who isn't used to living in a small town. You are local, aren't you?"

"Yes," Shari said. She didn't offer more information than that, and Mrs. Wallace didn't pry.

Shari walked ahead, holding back branches for Mrs. Wallace and taking the easiest route up to Eagle's Perch.

"You're quite a woodsman," Mrs. Wallace said with admiration when they stopped for her to catch her breath.

"I like the woods," Shari said and pointed to the tree whose thick arm reached out as if in judgment over the valley. In a crook between the two largest branches was the eagle's dishpan-sized nest of brown twigs.

"I owe you one for this," Mrs. Wallace said and promptly set about taking pictures. "My husband used to be the family photographer. This is his camera, much too fancy for a beginner like me, but I'm learning." She snapped pictures from a few different angles before buttoning her camera back into its case.

"Are you a fellow birder, Shari?"

"What?"

"Do you like to watch birds a lot?"

"Oh, yes."

"Seen any interesting ones besides this eagle?"

"I'm not too good at names," Shari said. "I try to look up what I see, but sometimes I forget the markings before I get to the library. I don't get there that often."

"Don't you have a Peterson's field guide?"

"No."

"Would you like one? I've got an extra. Cover's worn, but it's still good."

"Oh, no thank you."

"I'd like to give you something in exchange for showing me that nest."

"You don't have to."

"Tell you what—I'll leave the book at Mabel's store, and you can borrow it, keep it, or return it there as you like. You get to Mabel's store occasionally, don't you?"

"Everybody around here does."

"Yes, that's what I thought. Mabel's a friend of mine."

"I know."

Mrs. Wallace laughed. 'It's not fair for you to know so much about me when I don't know anything about you," she said.

The invitation to talk about herself made Shari uneasy. She dropped her eyes and looked away. She had already had a longer conversation with Mrs. Wallace than she had ever had with an adult at first meeting.

"You know," Mrs. Wallace said, "I'm going to need a guide to get me out of here. I don't have a clue which way to go except down."

"Just follow me," Shari said.

"Can you bring me out close to Mabel's store? That's where I left my car. Mabel's the one who told me about the eagle. My house looks off towards different mountains."

Shari nodded and struck off at a new angle down the mountains, leading Mrs. Wallace towards the Bravermans' land. They wouldn't object to two trespassers in their overgrown back fields, and passage in that direction would be easiest.

"Any time you want a recommendation as a mountain guide, just ask," Mrs. Wallace said when they emerged onto an old wagon road whose ruts were still not filled in with weeds.

"There used to be a house here," Shari said, turning away from the compliment, which pleased her nonetheless. "This is the Bravermans' place. Their grandfather lived here, but the house burned in a fire years ago." The crickets kept up a harsh, monotonous chirruping in the tough field grass around them. "See there." Shari pointed at the roofless building whose front door hung open at a drunken angle revealing a steep flight of stairs.

"Moo," a cow lowed plaintively. "*Moooooo.*"

Suddenly, three blond heads appeared around a blackberry patch that had hidden them. "There she goes again, Sue Ellen," a shrill voice piped. 'She's around here somewheres."

"In the house, Sue Ellen?" a girl identical to the first blond eight-year-old suggested.

"That old cow'd never fit through the front door," Sue Ellen said. Then she set her hands on her plump hips as she stared through the gaping entrance at the steep centre hall steps and said, "Well, I'll be! Look where that fool cow got to!"

The three Braverman girls hadn't noticed Shari and Mrs. Wallace because the blackberry patch had separated them, and when Mrs. Wallace called out, "Need any help?" Shari shrank back out of sight. She and Sue Ellen had been friends once, but no more. Despite Sue Ellen's womanly curves, she was thirteen and in the same grade as Shari at school.

"What's the matter, Shari?" Mrs. Wallace asked in a voice too low for Sue Ellen to hear. "Don't you want to help them?"

Since she saw no way out of it, Shari followed Mrs. Wallace over to the roofless house. Sue Ellen's eyes narrowed suspiciously when she saw Shari coming. "What are *you* doing around here?" Sue Ellen asked.

"Shari was guiding me back to the road," Mrs. Wallace said pleasantly. "What can we do for you?"

"Fool cow got herself up the stairs somehow, and now she don't know how to get down." They stood and surveyed the situation. The cow stood facing them at the top of the steps. Every once in a while it opened its big mouth to moo in distress. Its broad black-and-white face and pitiful expression were so ridiculous that Mrs.

Wallace grinned, and Shari found herself smiling too.

"It's not funny," Sue Ellen said sharply. "That's an expensive cow. She could break a leg on them stairs."

"You're right. I'm sorry," Mrs. Wallace said and got rid of all the laughter on her face except for the twinkle in her eyes.

Again Mrs. Wallace offered assistance.

"You could go tell my mother to call my father or the fire department," Sue Ellen said ungraciously. "We'll never get that cow out of here by ourselves."

"Right," Mrs. Wallace said. "Shari, do you know the way to this girl's house?"

"Sure she knows it," Sue Ellen said.

Shari turned in silence and began hurrying through the rusted farm machinery and broken bottles to the pasture. The downed, barbed-wire fence there explained the cow's escape route. When the bawling of the animal had diminished behind them, Mrs. Wallace asked, "Is that girl a friend of yours, Shari?"

"Not any more," Shari said. Again, Mrs. Wallace failed to pry. They hiked across the pasture, lumpy with tufts of grass, rocks and juniper bushes, towards the distant farmhouse.

It was too long and complicated a story to tell, Shari thought. Her relationship with Sue Ellen Braverman began way back when Charlotte and Sue Ellen's mother became girlhood enemies. "That woman's a gossip and a busybody," Charlotte had told Shari, "and don't you have anything to do with her daughter. I don't care if she's the only kid around here your age. I don't ever want her in this house and don't you go near hers neither."

Nevertheless, one day at break in first grade, Sue Ellen had said sensibly to Shari, "Listen, just 'cause our mamas don't like each other don't mean we can't be friends. Let's us be friends, Shari. Don't no one but us have to know about it."

Shari had warmed instantly to the idea of a secret friendship, and she'd been faithful to Sue Ellen in school and out, meeting her sometimes in Sue Ellen's grandfather's house to talk through sweet stolen hours or an afternoon. No matter that Shari hadn't been interested in the things Sue Ellen cared about. Listening had connected Shari to that larger world to which Sue Ellen belonged and given her the satisfaction of knowing she had a friend. By third grade, Sue Ellen had already added boys to her endless chatter about clothes and who said what mean thing to whom. She liked to elaborate on her dreams of getting married and having babies and owning a four-poster bed and an open-air swimming pool. Her only requirement of Shari was that she listen. Then one day, Sue Ellen noticed black-and-blue marks on Shari's arms.

"I bet it was Zeke done it," Sue Ellen said. At Shari's horrified denial, Sue Ellen had guessed, "Charlotte, then. It was your mother, wasn't it?"

"Don't tell anybody," Shari had gasped, and Sue Ellen had promised solemnly that her lips were sealed.

A few days later Shari discovered that every girl in her class was aware that her mother had beaten her. Sue Ellen was a person to avoid, not a friend at all.

For a while Sue Ellen acted as if she didn't care that

their friendship had ended. She had become friends with an older girl who had moved in nearby and no longer needed Shari anyway. After the older girl left town, Sue Ellen did try to renew her friendship with Shari, but when Shari remained cool to her, they became enemies. They were enemies still.

Mrs. Wallace reported the plight of the cow to Mrs. Braverman while Shari waited outside. The two of them resumed their progress towards the road. "It *was* a funny sight though, wasn't it?" Mrs. Wallace said. "That cow looked so bewildered. Too bad we can't see how they get her down those stairs."

"I wonder what made her climb up them," Shari said.

"Curiosity?" Mrs. Wallace suggested.

"A cow?"

"I guess not. Although I suspect most creatures have some curiosity in them. Anyway, I can see why that girl's not your friend. She's about as charming as the prickles on a blackberry bush."

Shari laughed and didn't deny it. She refused Mrs. Wallace's offer to buy her a lemonade or ice cream when they got to Mabel's store though, saying she had to get home. It was the truth.

"Well, Shari, you made my day," Mrs. Wallace said. "I'll send you that bird guide via Mabel, and if you should ever get a chance to stop by to see me, I hope you will."

Shari nodded, waved and hurried off. She knew Mrs. Wallace was just being polite. It would be nice to visit her, but Shari didn't expect she ever would.

That night Peter brought Shari his unopened bag of

potato chips and a candy bar, gifts of love from a boy who treasured food as much as he did. Immediately, she forgave him. "I had a good day too," she told him. "I climbed all the way to Eagle's Perch."

"You went without me?" he asked, as if it were she who had deserted him.

The next day it rained, and Zeke took them to Rutland where Charlotte went shopping for school clothes for them. While she was picking out shirts with the boys, Zeke walked Shari over to the girls' department. "Anything you want, honey. You pick it out and I'll pay for it," he said.

He was trying to make up for leaving her out of yesterday's fun, and she didn't want to hurt his feelings, but she'd never cared what she wore and had always been content to let Charlotte pick her clothes, with the exception of the too-big garage-sale dress in which Shari had felt so ugly.

"Mother will get me stuff," Shari said, looking around at the bewildering array of blouses and shirts and jeans and dresses and skirts. How did anyone know where to start?

Zeke looked puzzled. "I want to get you something special," he urged.

Shari squeezed his hand. "All I really want's a bird," she said. "And I know you can't get me that."

"I could, Shari, but I'd be in big trouble with your ma if I did."

"I know. It's all right."

"Tell you what. I'll see if I can find something extra

special for you next trip," he promised.

Another vest as pretty as the beaded Indian one that he'd brought her that Charlotte had given away? But Shari would never wear anything that unusual now. The last thing she wanted was to make herself stand out from the other girls.

"I don't need anything," she said. "I'm fine, Daddy."

"You're a good girl," he said, "the best any father could have."

She liked the compliment better than anything he could have bought her. It made a happy glow inside her all afternoon.

Six

The day before Zeke was going back on the road, he came into the kitchen for lunch and announced jovially, "Looks like Shari's getting a reward for returning that lady's property after all."

"What do you mean?" Charlotte asked. She was cutting up celery for the tuna-fish salad.

"Well, when I stopped at the store to pick up your cigarettes, Mabel told me Mrs. Wallace left a box there for Shari."

"Did you bring it?" Charlotte asked.

"No. You know Mabel. She's got her own way of doing things. She wants Shari to come get her gift herself."

"Can I go with you, Shari?" Peter asked and licked off his milk moustache in readiness.

"Sure you can."

Shari nibbled around and around her tuna-fish sandwich, leaving the soft, soggy centre for last while she tried to figure out how Mrs. Wallace could have found out who had returned her crystal swan. The fact that Mrs. Wallace had got her a gift wasn't surprising. It was the kind of thing she herself would have done if their positions were reversed.

Peter jiggled with excitement as they walked the quarter mile to the store. "I hope it's something to eat," he said.

"Maybe it's a box of candy," Shari said smiling. They swung their clasped hands in rhythm with their steps as they walked along the gravelly verge of the road out of the way of the cars swishing by. They passed Horner's farm with its big red barn and muddy yard and toy-sized cows pasted on the distant hillside field. Woods came next and then the small, square, white Pentecostal church with a black-lettered sign out front announcing Sunday services. The minister's topic was to be, "Leading the black sheep back to the fold." The duck pond was empty for a change, which meant the ducks had been carried off to market, still quacking, in slatted crates.

Across the way was Mabel's store with its petrol pump and saggy wooden porch decorated with boxes of empty lemonade bottles and an unopened crate of melons. "Vermont cheese" read the handwritten sign on one side of the glass-windowed front door; "Vermont maple syrup" read the sign on the other.

Mabel sold what was labelled penny candy from open glass jars on her counter, but she charged five cents a piece, or whatever she felt like that day. Sometimes she gave candy away free. Or she would bend her thin overalled length, extended by one of her pairs of dangling earrings, over the barrel of sunflower seeds and dip out a free bagful for Shari to feed to the birds. Mabel liked children. Her active, three-year-old grandson used the narrow aisles of the small store as roadways for his cars and lorries. Unwary shoppers were warned by Mabel to watch out that they didn't get run over.

"There you are!" Mabel called as soon as Shari stepped into the dim, cheesey-smelling interior. "Told your father to send you down here in a hurry. Look what was left here for you this morning!" She sounded as excited as if the surprise were for her as she handed Shari a small cardboard box with air holes. "Be careful how you peep inside, now. You don't want to let what's in there out."

"A bird," Shari said, unbelieving even as she lifted a corner of the top and peered into the box. "A blue parakeet!" Joy flooded her.

"Pretty little fella, ain't he?" Mabel leaned on the counter companionably.

"He's beautiful. He's the bluest blue. He's–beautiful." Shari, who rarely cried, found herself choking with tears.

Mabel popped the gum she was chewing. "Tickled pink, just like I thought she'd be," she said smugly.

"Let me see," Peter demanded. Shari held the box carefully to allow him to look inside.

"How did Mrs. Wallace know?" she asked.

"That you wanted a bird? Well, she asked me to find out what you'd like, so I asked Zeke, and he said a bird. He said your ma might not be too thrilled, but he thought she'd probably let you keep it once you got it."

"But how did Mrs. Wallace know it was me gave her back the crystal swan?" Shari asked.

"Oh, that was your ma. She come in here one morning and said how you'd returned the thing and been too shy to say anything. She said she thought you was owed a reward."

Suddenly Shari saw how it had worked out. Charlotte had done her a favour without meaning to, and Zeke had taken a chance for her sake. This time life hadn't been unfair, just tricky.

The bird scrabbled around in the box. "Let's get him home and let him out of there," Peter said. "Do you think Mama will let you keep him?"

"I don't know," Shari said, unwilling to consider any possible negatives.

Mabel insisted on closing her store and driving Shari and Peter and the bird home, even though Shari assured her that walking was no problem. "I'll go in with you in case your mother wants to know who to blame," Mabel said.

"Blame?" Peter asked. "What for?"

"With your ma, you can never tell," Mabel said.

She pulled her car up in their drive and followed Shari and Peter to the kitchen door. "Yoo hoo," she called. "Charlotte, come and see what Eve Wallace got Shari as a reward."

"It's a parakeet, Mama," Peter said. "He's blue with a white head and a black ring around his eye."

Charlotte stood in the doorway with a lit cigarette in her mouth. She took a puff, staring at the box, and asked, "What kind of reward is that?"

"A good one for a girl who likes birds," Mabel said.

"And who told Mrs. Wallace Shari likes birds?"

"I guess it must've been me," Mabel said thoughtfully.

"I remember Shari was always coming in for birdseed last year, and didn't *you* tell me how bad she felt when it died on her?"

"She left the window open, and it flew away," Charlotte said.

"Is that what happened? Well, I'm sure she'll take better care of this little fella," Mabel said cheerfully. "Anyway a bird's no trouble, and Shari's a year older and wiser."

Charlotte frowned at the box and said nothing.

Mabel grinned and winked at Shari. "I'll tell Eve Wallace how pleased you are."

"I'm going to thank her myself," Shari said.

Good idea. Want a lift up there tomorrow afternoon? Her and I usually visit Thursday afternoons when my Charley takes over the store for me."

"I don't need a ride, but thank you for the offer, Mabel."

"You're not gonna *walk* that far? It's got to be three or four miles, child," Mabel objected.

"Not the way I go. I know a shortcut."

"Well, suit yourself."

Mabel explained to Charlotte that Mrs. Wallace had also paid for a year's worth of birdseed and gravel as part of her gift to Shari. "Ain't that nice?"

"Mmmmmmm." Charlotte's eyes narrowed as she took short, quick puffs on her cigarette.

When Mabel drove off with a farewell toot of her horn, Shari looked straight at her mother and said, "Thank you very much."

"For what?"

"For not making me give back the bird."

"Why would I do that? Just be sure it doesn't make a mess in your room. And this time, keep your window shut."

Shari didn't say anything. She wondered if Charlotte could truly have forgotten who opened that window last summer.

Peter closed Shari's bedroom door and Shari made sure the screen on her window was latched before she transferred the bird to the old cage that had stood empty all year. She filled the water and feeder cups and lined the cage with notebook paper, while the parakeet huddled fearfully on a dowel perch in the cage with its feathers fluffed out.

"What are you going to call him?" Peter asked.

"Blue Boy," Shari said without hesitation.

"I thought it was Zeke told Mabel you wanted a bird," Peter said while they waited for Blue Boy to adjust to his new environment. "But Mabel didn't say it that way to Mama. Mabel said *she* was the one told Mrs. Wallace you—"

"What's the difference?" Shari asked. "As long as I can keep Blue Boy, that's all that matters."

"But why did Mabel tell us it was Daddy told her and tell Mama different?"

"Peter," Shari said earnestly, "don't talk about it, huh? And if you want to play with Blue Boy, be sure you don't leave my door or window open so he can fly out of this room."

"You don't have to tell me that," he said. "Think I'm dumb or something?"

Just then Blue Boy jumped to the swing in the centre of the cage and rocked gently back and forth. He ducked his head and chirped throatily. Then he began to cluck and squawk as if he were talking out his version of his day's adventures. Shari watched him blissfully.

Peter got bored and left her alone with her bird long before Blue Boy had drunk from his water cup, scattered seed from his feeder everywhere and made a watery grey-and-white deposit on the floor of his cage. She poked a finger through the bars to offer him as a perch, and he pecked at her, but gently. The afternoon sailed by, and suddenly Charlotte was calling her to come down and help get supper ready.

The next morning, Blue Boy sat on Shari's finger, his wiry claws clasped around it, as she promised to buy him a cuttlebone and repeated his name over and over, telling him what a pretty, pretty Blue Boy he was.

"Happy with your bird?" Zeke asked her when she ran downstairs to say goodbye to him.

"Yes," she told him as she kissed his clean-shaven face, although the sight of his packed bag near the door brought on the lurch of despair she usually felt when it was time for him to leave again. Charlotte clung to him and cried as she always did. Doug and Walter had already gone to their stand for the day.

"Come back soon, Daddy, and bring me some chocolate-chip cookies this time," Peter said.

They waved goodbye as Zeke's big cab backed out of the drive and onto the road heading for the furniture factory where he was to pick up his next load.

Charlotte wiped her eyes and headed for the telephone to wring some comfort from her friends. "You kids stay out of my hair today," she said over her shoulder.

Already the sun was hot, even though it was still morning. No clouds to mar the purity of sky above the basking mountains. "I'm going to visit Mrs. Wallace and thank her," Shari told Peter. "Do you want to stay here with Mama or come with me?"

"Mama told you to call Mrs. Wallace up and thank her when she sent the bird book. Only you didn't," Peter said. "You could call her now and thank her twice and we wouldn't have to hike all that way."

"If you don't want to come, stay home then," Shari said.

"You're not afraid to use the phone, are you, Shari? Mama said you were afraid to use the phone."

"I don't like to use it," Shari admitted.

"Why not? I don't mind," Peter said.

"I just don't like to," Shari said and tried to explain. "You can't see what people are thinking on the telephone. It's only their voice from a machine. . . . Anyway, you should meet Mrs. Wallace, Peter. She's a nice lady."

"You just like her because she likes birds."

"Mabel says she makes her own jam and bread too," Shari coaxed.

"Will she give us some?" Peter sounded more interested.

"I don't know, and don't you embarrass me by asking her."

"I wouldn't do that," Peter said. "I'm not such a baby."

Once they were through the ravine, the road to Mrs. Wallace's seemed shorter than it had the last time Shari had walked it with Peter. They found Mrs. Wallace weeding her vegetable garden. She looked up when Shari called hello and said, "Shari! How nice that you came. I was just thinking about you."

"This is Peter, my little brother," Shari said.

"And how are you on this hot summer morning, Peter?" Mrs. Wallace asked.

"Thirsty," Peter said promptly.

"Peter!" Shari scolded.

"I didn't ask. I just answered," Peter said.

At that, Mrs. Wallace laughed so heartily that tears came to her eyes. "Let's go inside for an iced-tea break," she said when she could talk again. "It's too hot to weed all this lettuce anyway. I should have mulched it better. . . . Do butter cookies and lemonade sound good to you, Peter?"

"Yeah!" he said with enthusiasm and glanced at Shari to see if she disapproved.

"Peter likes to eat," Shari said apologetically.

"Nothing wrong with that," Mrs. Wallace said. "I'm very fond of good food myself." She led them into a kitchen so crosshatched with sunlight that the details faded into the brightness. Shari saw plants and hanging pots and onions on a string hooked to an overhead beam.

A staircase with a sinewy handrail made of polished tree branches ran up one side of the room. On the other side of the stairs was a red brick wall. Mrs. Wallace gave Shari the job of squeezing the lemons, while Peter was set to placing cookies from the jar onto a plate.

"I came to say thank you," Shari said. "For the beautiful bird and for lending me the bird book."

"It's not a loan," Mrs. Wallace said. "You may keep the book, and I'm glad you like the bird. What did you name him?"

"Blue Boy," Shari said.

"Nice name. I hope he gives you as much pleasure as you gave me by returning that crystal swan. It was one of the last gifts from my husband, and I treasured it especially."

"It's beautiful," Shari said.

Mrs. Wallace helped herself to a cookie and offered Shari iced tea. Shari asked if she could try the lemonade that Peter was having instead.

"It's good," Peter said. "Better than from the can."

"And are you a bird lover like your sister and me, Peter?" Mrs. Wallace asked.

"No, I like trucks," he said.

"Peter wants to be a truck driver like our father," Shari said.

"Or I could get a hamburger stand maybe," Peter offered.

"And eat up all your own hamburgers?" Mrs. Wallace asked.

"Not all. Some of them I'd sell."

Mrs. Wallace smiled. "Shari, you know what I've been thinking about? Do you know anything about bird banding?"

"Is it something to do with keeping track of migrating birds?"

"Yes, and a way of keeping a rough census on the various kinds of birds and their life spans. Banding has lots of purposes. You need to get a licence from the U.S. Fish and Wildlife Service first, and then, if you're on a migratory route as we are here, you can set up nets in the spring and autumn to catch the birds just long enough to clamp little metal tags on one of their legs.

"Of course, it's important to keep good records. Eventually, the information is recorded on a central computer and used for the preservation of birds and their environments. It's a big responsibility to be an official bird bander, and if I start, I'd need to keep at it. I'm not sure I could handle it by myself."

"Could I help you?" Shari asked. "I mean, if there's something I could do—"

"I was hoping you'd say that." Mrs. Wallace looked happy.

"Is it a job? Are you going to pay her?" Peter asked.

"Well, it's a job, but the volunteer kind, Peter," Mrs. Wallace said. "People don't usually get paid for bird banding. Although I could give Shari—"

"No, no," Shari said. "I wouldn't want to get paid. It would be fun for me."

"Why do you want to work without getting paid?" Peter asked. "Doug wouldn't, and Mama says it's stupid to work for nothing, like she does in the house."

"Mama doesn't work for nothing. She works to raise us and please Zeke, and Zeke takes care of her and loves her in return."

"Actually, working for love is better than working for money," Mrs. Wallace told Peter. "It's more satisfying to a person."

"I don't get it," Peter said.

"Well, let's see if I can explain it," Mrs. Wallace said. "Lots of important jobs are done for free just because people want to do them. Take people who visit patients in hospitals to cheer them up, and flower arrangement ladies who beautify their towns with flowers, and volunteers who pile up sandbags to keep rivers from flooding. Lots of things that make life better society can't afford to pay for. Raising children is another good example."

"But if you don't get paid, you won't get any money," Peter argued. "And Doug says you got to have a lot of money to live good."

Mrs. Wallace looked amused. "Well, most people don't spend *all* their time on volunteer activities," she said, "just whatever time they can afford."

"Shari can't afford any. She can't even afford to go to school and be a pilot," Peter said.

"Is that your ambition, Shari?" Mrs. Wallace asked.

"She wants to fly a jet plane," Peter said.

"My father told me you have to go to school to be a pilot," Shari said, looking at Mrs. Wallace for confirmation.

"It's true you need training," Mrs. Wallace said. "But I

believe if you join one of the services, like the air force, they'll send you to school and train you, so long as you're physically and mentally capable of doing the job."

"And you don't have to pay for it?"

"Not if you enlist. I think they require you to serve a certain number of years in exchange for your education. Of course, the danger is if there's a war—"

"But you could really be a pilot without having any money?" Shari interrupted eagerly.

"I believe so," Mrs. Wallace said.

Shari's smile stretched out her cheeks.

"She didn't know that," Peter explained unnecessarily, and grandly told his sister, "I guess you might as well help Mrs. Wallace band the birds, Shari, if you don't need to earn no money."

"Thanks, Pete," she said. "I'm glad you approve."

She was teasing, but he nodded, taking her seriously. "I do," he said.

"Well, we'll talk about the bird banding some more once I investigate it a little further and see what we're getting into," Mrs. Wallace said. "It would be nice to have an excuse to see more of you, Shari."

"And me too?" Peter asked.

"'The cookie jar will always be out for you, my friend," Mrs. Wallace promised solemnly. Shari laughed, but Peter looked pleased.

It was only a few days later that Charlotte told Shari Mrs. Wallace had called. "She said she wanted to talk to you about some project with birds you and her are going to do together. She said she got a mass of material from the government and she wants to know how much time you're gonna have once school starts. I told her you got no time to go running around after birds. You got plenty to do here for me, and you don't do half of what you should as is."

"I can just go when you don't need me," Shari said.

"Yeah, well, if you want to spend your free time with that crazy lady—"

"She's not crazy."

"No? Going around catching birds and putting bands on their legs sounds crazy to me."

"But it's okay if I go to talk to her about it, isn't it?"

"You want to go climbing around in this heat, go ahead. Just be sure you and your brother stay out of my hair. After I clean out the refrigerator, I've got a pile of mending to do, and Doug's trousers need letting out again."

Peter was playing outside when Shari went to ask him if he wanted to go along with her to Mrs. Wallace's.

"It's too hot to walk all that way," Peter said. "I want to play cement mixer in the pool with my trucks."

"All right then. I'll be back later."

Today Shari was glad to leave without him and hurried off before he had a chance to change his mind. She could move faster alone.

The heat brought out the green leafy scent of the woods. Shari breathed deeply of it as she slipped through the lacy sun and shadows under the trees, down into the cool damp of the ravine where the stream burbled slowly over the rocks and even the rapids' roar seemed muted. Up the steep side, over the projecting ledge—in no time, she had arrived breathless at the edge of Mrs. Wallace's lawn. Shari halted there, locked tight in a fit of shyness by the sight of Mrs. Wallace sitting on her front steps shelling peas.

The head with the neat, white cap of hair lifted and wise eyes found Shari. Mrs. Wallace's round cheeks puffed up in a smile as she said, "There's my young friend. Come sit beside me here in the shade while I finish shelling these peas."

"May I help?"

"You certainly may. Shelling peas is dull work to do alone," Mrs. Wallace said.

Shari relaxed in the warmth of Mrs. Wallace's welcome. She broke a pod into the colander of peas on the stone step between Mrs. Wallace's ample hip and her own slim one, thinking how much she liked this lady.

"I don't know why I grow so many peas," Mrs. Wallace said. "Certainly can't eat them all, and it's a shame to waste them. How about doing me a favour and taking some home to your family?"

"Oh, no thank you," Shari responded with her usual reluctance to take gifts from someone she didn't know very well. Accepting gifts from strangers was taking charity, Charlotte and Zeke had taught her, unless you had something to give in exchange. "My mother said you wanted to talk to me about the bird banding."

"Your mother didn't sound too enthused about our project."

"She isn't. She thinks birds aren't worth wasting my time on."

"My good friend Mabel would agree. Mabel says it takes a pair of odd ducks like you and me to get more pleasure out of feathered creatures than our own two-legged kind." Mrs. Wallace's lips quirked with a held-back grin. "That's Mabel for you. She thinks I'm in danger of becoming a hermit. I expect you're too young for her to accuse you of that yet."

"What's wrong with hermits?" Shari asked.

"Nothing. I've met ones as nice or nicer than other people, just not as social."

"I watched you before I returned your swan," Shari confessed. "I saw you let that sparrow hawk go."

"Did you?"

"It was wonderful," Shari said with feeling.

Mrs. Wallace's clear grey eyes lit in a smile. "Letting wild creatures go free when they can take care of themselves is an act of respect. I found that hawk flopping around the woods with one damaged wing and fed him for the couple of weeks it took him to heal. That's all. It was beautiful, wasn't it, the way he circled up at the top of the sky as if he never planned to come back down?"

"I like hawks best," Shari said, and hastened to add in case she'd insulted Mrs. Wallace, "I mean, to watch outdoors. Inside I like parakeets. . . . I don't think Blue Boy minds being caged too much."

"Probably not. Anyway, a tropical bird like him would never survive a northern winter outside. That's for sure."

"I had another parakeet. He flew out of my bedroom

window last summer and he never came back. I suppose—" She swallowed and left her sentence trembling between them. It was tempting to tell Mrs. Wallace things. She listened patiently as if she cared. Shari had the feeling that Mrs. Wallace would understand even those closed-box secrets she'd hidden from herself, but she couldn't risk letting them out even so. Who knew what monstrous forms they had taken back there in the dark attic of her mind!

"What I need," Shari said dreamily, "is to be a bird or, anyway, some kind of flyer so I can leave the earth behind like the sparrow hawk did."

"You don't find the earth beautiful enough to hold you?"

Shari shrugged. "It's beautiful; it's just that I need to get away from it sometimes."

"What do you need to get away from particularly?"

"Things," Shari said and was relieved when Mrs. Wallace didn't press her further.

"As to wanting to be a bird—" Mrs. Wallace paused to consider it. "There you and I differ. A bird's wings could never provide me with half the adventure my human mind gets from reading and learning and thinking. A bird can only explore the visible world, at least so far as we know, but our minds can go where no creatures have ever been and into the past and on to the future." Mrs. Wallace's smile lifted all the curves of her plain face. "Now how about some lemonade to wash down that heavy dose of philosophy?" she said.

After the lemonade, Mrs. Wallace had to show Shari

the oriole's nest hanging like a small, round mailbag from a branch of the cherry tree. Next she told Shari the saga of the tiny wrens who'd chased the larger sparrows away from a birdhouse in which the wrens had nested the year before. "They won, those little wrens, just by sheer force of character," Mrs. Wallace said.

She told Shari about her granddaughters, Christine and Jackie, and how Jackie was away at soccer camp because she hoped to be a professional ball player when she grew up, and Chris had a job as a mother's helper this year. "I expect to see them in the autumn," Mrs. Wallace said, "but I do miss their summer visit. The truth is, I enjoy young people more than adults, except for Mabel."

"I never knew my grandparents," Shari said. "They died in a car crash right on the highway near Mabel's store. Then my mother was raised by her grandparents, but I never knew them either. They moved down to Florida when my mother married Zeke and they died down in Florida—I don't know what of—but they never came back here even for a visit. My mother had a fight with them or something."

"Maybe they didn't want her to marry Zeke."

"I don't see how that could be. Everybody likes Zeke. He's so good. He worked at the garage where my mother's grandparents got their car serviced, but the garage went out of business; so Zeke had to work at a meat-packing place in Rutland. He didn't like that job much."

"It must be hard for you to have your father on the road all the time."

"Yes, I miss him a lot."

"I bet your mother does too."

"Yes, she misses him."

"She's very young to have so many children."

"Oh, she's not as young as she looks. She's thirty-one," Shari said.

Mrs. Wallace laughed and said, "That's very young, Shari. Mabel says your mother had you and then your two older brothers all before she was twenty."

"I know," Shari said quickly. "But why'd she have us if she didn't want us?" She blushed, embarrassed at what she'd blurted out.

"Lots of women seem pretty vague about reproduction. They just get pregnant without thinking much about it. Anyway, if she doesn't have any more children, she could go out and get herself a job and that might make her happier."

"She won't have any more children," Shari said, remembering the weeks of nagging Charlotte had gone through to talk Zeke into having a vasectomy after Peter was born. "But I don't think she'll ever get a job."

"Why not?"

"She keeps making excuses."

"People do change, Shari."

"I suppose so." She couldn't imagine Charlotte changing. "What time is it, Mrs. Wallace?"

When Shari discovered that three hours had passed since she'd left home, she was dismayed. "I'd better go now," she said. "Peter must be wondering where I am."

"You don't mind being in charge of him so much at all,

do you?" Mrs. Wallace asked.

"Mind? Oh, no. Peter and I are a pair."

Mrs. Wallace nodded as if she understood. It gave Shari pleasure to be so quickly understood.

She was on her way and almost out of earshot when Mrs. Wallace called, "Shari! I completely forgot to show you all that material on bird banding I got in the mail."

"I'll come back soon," Shari answered. "Maybe tomorrow."

Even before she had swung over the protruding lip above the ravine, she wished she hadn't said it. Being too sure of anything was risky. Expecting good luck sometimes brought on bad. She should have known from past experience never to take anything for granted, she thought despairingly at the sight of the red tee shirt in the bottom of the ravine.

She slipped and skidded down the steep gravelled side and bent over Peter's still body. He was lying face down where he'd fallen, close to the stream.

"Petey?" He didn't move. "Petey?" She touched him. His body was warm, but his stillness terrified her. "Petey?" His eyes were closed and his face was smeared with blood and dirt. She remembered learning that you weren't supposed to move people if they had had a bad fall. Carefully she put her ear to his chest and held her breath. When she heard his heart beat, she left him lying there and raced across the log and up the ravine, running for home and help as fast as her fear could propel her.

Seven

Charlotte's wail made the disaster real to Shari.

"Peter's lying hurt in the bottom of the ravine," Shari had announced. Now she had to force herself past her screaming mother to the telephone, where Zeke had pasted emergency numbers for fire and police and the rescue squad. Tension made Shari's fingers so stiff that she had difficulty dialling, but finally the call went through. "My brother needs help," she said and briefly described where Peter had fallen. Charlotte yanked the phone from her hands to add a garbled plea for them to hurry.

Shari started back out to her brother, but Charlotte stopped her. "Don't you dare leave this house. You stay here and wait for Doug and Walter. I'll take care of Peter."

"But you don't know where he is and I do."

"I told you. Stay here," Charlotte said. Each word burned with hate as she added, "Do like I say for once. I'm going to my son now and I'll deal with you later."

Shari heard her mother starting her car. If Charlotte waited for the rescue squad at the bridge that crossed high over the ravine and directed them from there, they would enter the ravine too far from Peter. With no path to follow and rocks and brambles to hold them back, they'd take forever to get to him. Suppose Peter opened his eyes and found himself alone! Shari couldn't obey. She couldn't remain in the house doing nothing when Peter might need her.

She began running back along the short-cut. He was still unconscious when she reached him. She couldn't tell by listening for a heartbeat if he was alive or not because her breath was coming in gasps and her own heart pounded too loudly in her ears. Blood oozed from his hair. When she put her arms around him, he felt suspiciously cool. She kissed him and spoke to him and tried warming him with her body. Once she thought she saw his eyelids flutter, but she couldn't be sure.

"Petey, wake up. Petey, I love you so much. Please be all right," she begged. Sitting there on the damp ground, she shivered. How much colder he must feel! She wanted to get his body off the ground and onto her lap, but she was afraid to risk moving him. All she could do was wait. She didn't cry. She was too full of dread to cry.

She listened in the dark at the bottom of the ravine while the water warbled its way over the rocks and birds whistled to each other across the stream until, at last, she heard the voices of the rescue squad. "You see him anywheres?" "Not yet." "Think we're in the right place?"

"Here!" Shari yelled. "He's here, here, here." Her voice echoed. She kept screaming until she was hoarse and an answer came back.

"Okay, we hear you."

A lanky, grey-haired man and a chunky young woman in jeans came crashing through the thicket on the far bank. "There's a log you can cross the stream on," Shari yelled.

She heard them curse and encourage each other as they eased their way across. Then they were there to take charge. She felt hopeful now. They would take care of Peter.

"Is there a better way out than how we came in?" the woman asked Shari as the man wrapped Peter in a blanket and secured him to a stretcher.

"Kid's in shock," the man said softly.

"I'll show you the way. Follow me," Shari said and took off.

"Would've been easier if we'd known this route in the first place," the man said when she'd led them out. "You're some climber, honey, a first-class mountain goat."

Mourning doves cried sadly in the trees as they emerged into the late-afternoon sunlight. The man used his walkie-talkie to call the ambulance to meet them at the house. Charlotte drove up behind the ambulance and got in as they bundled Peter inside. They raced off with siren screaming.

Walter and Doug got home anxious to know what had happened. They'd been told by neighbours that their brother had been killed.

"He's in shock," Shari said. "He'll be all right." She didn't know what shock was, except it was something that people lived through, came out of, something that passed.

"Where's Ma?" Doug asked.

"She went in the ambulance with Pete."

"You going to make supper?" Walter asked.

"No," Shari said. "You can make yourselves sandwiches if you're hungry." She was tired. Even her bones were tired, and her head hurt as if in sympathy with Peter's. The unfamiliar urge to cry overtook her.

She dragged up to her room and got an enthusiastic greeting from Blue Boy, who gripped the bars of his cage and bobbed his head and chattered as if he were questioning her. Wasn't she going to talk to him? Where had she been, leaving him alone so long? She looked at him helplessly and threw herself on her bed, choking on unshed tears.

Hours later she was sitting by the window in the dark listening to the intricate details of night business outside when a car stopped in front of the house and Charlotte's voice came clearly thanking someone for the ride. The door to the house closed. Shari stiffened. She thought of getting into bed and pretending to be asleep, but knew better than to hope she could escape her mother's wrath that way. She waited for the sound of Charlotte's footsteps on the stairs and held her breath as her mother stopped outside her door. One frightened part of Shari wanted to hide, and another part held fast to her old protective shield. Nothing can hurt me, that part of her said. No matter what she does, she can't touch me inside. Only this time, Peter was involved and that made Shari vulnerable. He had lain there so still with the blood on his face and in his hair. Waves of panic hit her just thinking of how still he had lain.

The door opened. Shari glanced at her mother's face, but she couldn't read it. Charlotte's expression was set in hard, tired lines with none of the prettiness that she showed Zeke.

"Aren't you going to ask about your brother?" Charlotte said. "Don't you want to know how he is?"

"Is he all right?"

"How could he be after what you did to him?"

"I didn't do anything."

"You took him down there to play, didn't you?"

"No, not today. He came by himself. I went to Mrs. Wallace's, and he didn't want to come with me, so I left him at home. Then he must have changed his mind or something."

"You left him home?"

"You were here."

"I should have known better than to trust you with him. You've always been a rotten mean kid since the day you were born. Never a smile out of you. Never a hug or a kiss. Soon as you could walk, you ran away from me, never to me, always away. I thought you had feelings for him at least, but you let him fall down that ravine, and if he dies, you just better believe it was you who killed him." She turned around and left, shutting first Shari's door and then her own behind her.

Shari crept to her bed and pulled the covers over her head. Inside her, everything was shattered ice. She couldn't get warm. One hope only stood out in the white glare of her mother's hatred. He wasn't dead yet. He hadn't died. And tomorrow, no matter what, Shari would go to the hospital and see him.

In the morning, Shari took care of Blue Boy first. As she cleaned out his cage, he sat on her shoulder, puffed out his throat feathers and ducked his head, chirping and squawking at her. She set out a dish of water for his bath in the bottom of his clean cage. He balanced in the doorway, which she'd fixed open by attaching it to the cage with a paper clip.

While he considered whether to bathe or not, she went about getting herself dressed for the visit to the hospital. She had to look old enough so they'd let her in. She didn't own a skirt, but she had a blouse with small pink rosebuds and a little round collar that would do, and she tied her hair back with a pink ribbon from a birthday package. Her sneakers were dirty, but she didn't have time to wash them.

Money. After someone had raised the glass jar in which she collected her money, she had begun to hide the occasional allowance Zeke gave her, and now she had to think for a minute to recall where the last hiding place had been. In an envelope stuck to the back of her dresser drawer, she remembered, and eased the drawer out as quietly as she could. The envelope was there but it held only two dollars. She couldn't buy transportation with that, but she could get Petey some candy or cookies when she got to town. First, before she risked hitching, she'd see if Mabel had any deliveries going from the store in the right direction.

The house was quiet when Shari slipped out of her room. Her family was still sleeping. Her stomach reminded her that she hadn't eaten last night. In fact, she couldn't recall whether she'd had lunch yesterday or not. She'd better stop to eat something before she left, maybe take a sandwich with her in case she was gone all day.

She left a note on the kitchen table: "Went to see Peter." She didn't sign it, "Love." There was no love, had never been any according to what Charlotte said last night. From the moment of her birth, her mother had hated her. She wondered if she was feelingless as Charlotte claimed. The truth was, nobody mattered to her besides Peter now, and what she felt for him was cold fear, nothing as warm and caressing as love. Even Zeke seemed beyond range of her feelings. Except Shari wished he were here. He wouldn't blame her for Peter's fall, and Charlotte would be less dangerous if Zeke were home.

In her hurry, Shari dropped the peanut-butter jar. It didn't break, but rolled noisily on the vinyl floor, and when she finished making her sandwich and was ready to go, a voice said, "You little sneak. Where do you think you're going all dressed up?"

"To the hospital. I left you a note," Shari said quickly.

Charlotte stood there puffy faced in her transparent lavender nightgown. "You're not going nowhere," she said. "After what you did to him, you're not going near him. I told them not to let you into the hospital."

Shari knew it was a lie as soon as the words left her

mother's mouth. "I'll tell Zeke if you don't let me go," Shari blurted out.

"You'll do what?" Charlotte took a step towards her, eyes fierce. "What did you say to me? You'll do what?" She took another menacing step towards Shari.

"I know you don't love me," Shari said. "But Zeke does. He'll understand about Peter." She gasped and her hand went automatically to her head where her mother had knocked it against the corner of the kitchen cabinet. Blood oozed through her hair as her mother slapped her cheek, so hard that Shari fell down. Charlotte grabbed her and jerked her up, gripping her arms so that Shari couldn't protect her face, but Charlotte didn't want to hit her again.

"You think Zeke loves you?" Charlotte hissed into Shari's face. "You know how funny that is? Why would he love you when you're not even his own kid? How do you think you got to be such a narrow, skinny little rat? It's because you look like your father, that's how come. Just because Zeke lets you use his name don't mean he's your father. Your father ran away as soon as he found out I was pregnant. Not that I lost anything when I lost him. He wasn't much, let me tell you, about as loving as a rat, and you were born just like him." She shoved Shari away from her. "Now you go upstairs to your room and you stay there until I say you can come out, and don't you ever threaten to tell on me to Zeke again. Don't you ever dare."

Charlotte stood watching as Shari fumbled her way to the stairs, swaying a little, having to lean against the wall as she climbed to keep her balance. Shari crept into her room. Blue Boy was vigorously flicking water drops from his bath in all directions. He fussed with his feathers, stretched out a wing, groomed it with his beak and then did the other. She watched him for a minute, but then she had to lie down on her bed. Her hair felt sticky from the blood oozing from the bump, which was swelling. Her cheek stung where Charlotte had slapped her, but the physical pain was outside her. Deep inside was the raw, burning hole Charlotte's direct hit had torn. The father whose love had given Shari all the comfort and reassurance there had been in life was gone, cut off from her as surely as if he were dead. Suddenly, Shari saw herself alone, not by her own choice, but by the chance of birth that had brought her to a mother who hated her and no father at all. A suffocating loneliness overcame her, shutting out thought, making it hard for her to breathe.

When her mind began to function again, it was only to deal with the immediate, the problem of how she would get to Peter. Patiently, she tried to reason it out, but each thought slipped away as she reached for it. Walter and Doug were stirring, getting up, going downstairs. Blue Boy rested on his swing looking content with himself as the bright morning sun lit up his cage. The patch of sky in the top corner of her window promised a perfect summer day. Still Shari lay on her bed, too groggy to move.

Someone knocked at her door. "Who is it?" she asked.

The door opened and Walter stuck his head in "She's gone to the hospital," he said. "She said she'll be gone all day. You want anything?"

"No, thank you."

He waited, then he said, "Well, if you want anything, I'll get it for you before Doug and me go to his stand.... I could lend you a book."

"Did she tell you how Peter is?"

"He's got a concussion," she said. I don't know what that means."

"Me neither." He kept standing there, so she smiled at him for his kindness, for stepping out of his normal indifference to try to help her.

Awkwardly, he shifted from one foot to the other. "Well, if you need anything . . ." he said and waited.

"Nothing, thanks." Finally he left.

The problem of how to get around Charlotte's presence in Peter's hospital room and find out if was all right lay snarled in Shari's mind. At last she began to untangle it. Mabel—she always heard everything. Shari could get her to call and find out from Charlotte how Peter really was.

Shari got to her feet and down the stairs and out of the empty house. She walked down the road, so intent on getting to Mabel's store that she barely noticed her physical discomfort. The story was empty. Mabel was sitting on the porch reading a western from the paperback rack, her reading glasses halfway down her long nose, earrings dangling, long hair pulled back and curling on her forehead, and one long thin leg crossed over the other and swinging rhythmically.

"What's the matter, Shari honey? You look done in," Mabel said looking over the tops of her glasses.

"Have you heard about Peter?"

"I'll say I did. Poor little fella. I was here when the ambulance went roaring by. What happened to your face?"

"Nothing," Shari asked. "Mabel, do you think you could call my mother and ask how Peter is?"

"Call your mother? Where is she? Oh, sure, don't mind me. She must've went to the hospital."

"Yes," Shari said. "Could you call and ask about Peter? I mean, like it's *you* wants to know. Don't tell her it's me asking."

"Why not?" Mabel's homely face knotted in confusion.

"Because she's mad at me," Shari said and shrugged and tried to smile as her eyes fell away.

"You don't mean she blames you for what happened to Peter?"

Shari nodded.

"Well, that's nonsense. She'll get over that. Don't you worry, honey. You're the best big sister any boy could have. You just can't be holding on to him every single minute, that's all; and boys will get into trouble the minute you turn your back on them. Want me to tell her that?"

"No. Please, don't say anything about me at all. Please? Just call and ask how Peter is."

"Ummmm." Mabel reached out bony fingers to touch Shari's cheek. "That's some nasty bruise you've got. Looks like whoever you were fighting got you good. And what's that on your head?"

Shari drew back. "It's nothing. I'm all right. Please call, Mabel."

"Sure, I can do that easy enough. Come inside. Want a lemonade? It's on the house." Mabel went to the phone on the wall at the back of the store. While she was dialling, Shari stood before the glass-fronted cooler looking at the stacks of colourful cans and bottles inside. A wave of dizziness washed over her. The peanut-butter sandwich probably still lay on the kitchen floor where it had fallen when Charlotte grabbed her.

". . . Well, if there's no telephone in the room, could you get Mrs. Lally to call Mabel at the store, please?" Mabel said into the phone. A few seconds later she hung up and said, "Come sit outside with me a minute, Shari. Your ma will likely call back."

Shari asked if she might take a pint container of milk instead of lemonade.

"Sure. You *are* looking peaked, child. Have one of these doughnuts too. I already opened the package to treat myself this morning. . . . Shari? Are you all right?"

When Shari came to, Mabel told her she had fainted. "Your mother called, and I told her how you was so worried you'd come down here and had me call to find out how your little brother was doing, and then you'd fainted right away. Scared me half to death passing out like that. . . . Here, sip some of this cold milk. Not too many sisters dote on their little brothers the way you do on Peter, I told her. I don't think she's mad at you any more. She said—Are you feeling better now? Don't move; just sip the milk slow and easy. Shocks will do that to you—make the blood run clear out of your head. I fainted once myself—would you believe it, big as I am? Fainted in the doctor's office when they stitched up my little grandson. He didn't pass out; I did." She laughed at herself.

"What did she say about Peter?" Shari asked wearily. Mabel had done her in by letting Charlotte know that Shari had left the house. Mabel had just got rattled and talked. She hadn't understood at all why Shari didn't want her to tell. Better not to think about the consequences she'd have to face when Charlotte got home.

"Peter's doing all right, just fine," Mabel said. "A little woozy from the concussion that's all."

"But he's awake? He's not unconscious any more?"

"Well, I don't know. Must be awake. Anyway, she said to tell you to go home and wait for her there. She'll be back by supper time."

"She's not bringing Peter home?"

"Not yet, honey. But don't you worry. He's got a head hard as a rock, that little fella. He'll be just fine. Looks like you got hit on the head yourself. Did you do that yesterday? When you was in the ravine?"

"I . . . don't know," Shari said.

Mabel sighed. "Sometimes," she said kindly, "when a parent gets riled, they strike out at whoever's around. My papa used to backhand us every once in a while, hit us so hard our ears would ring, and he'd keep on walking just like he'd never done a thing. It taught us to be careful how we acted around him, but he didn't mean us no harm. Just wanted to see we were brought up good and proper. Your mama's grandma—you know, the one who raised Charlotte—she had a heavy hand, believed a good spanking cured a lot of things."

"I'd better get back home," Shari said.

"How about if I give you a lift?"

"No, thank you. I can walk."

"Nonsense," Mabel said. "I'll just shut the store for a few minutes and take you home." Without giving Shari a chance to argue, she flipped the sign on the door to CLOSED and shut the door behind them as she ushered Shari out to the car parked in front.

"You've got a nice family," Mabel said as she backed out of the drive. "Doug and Walter are such good, hard-working boys, and Zeke is as steady a fella as anybody could want for a father, but your mama's a little on the nervous side, and she's alone with the four of you too much. You got to be a good child and help her and maybe not go running off in the woods all the time like she complains you do."

Shari heard Mabel's words, but they bounced off her as if Mabel were talking about some other family. The only one Shari still felt bound to was Peter. The others had been cut off from her. More than ever before in her life, she was outside, apart and alone.

Mabel stopped the car in Shari's drive and looked at her. "You know, your mama was a real goody-goody little girl growing up," Mabel said and went rambling on. "Her grandmother was just as proud of how well behaved and neat and sweet she was. Of course, when Charlotte got to high school, she made up for it. Used to cut school and fool around where she oughtn't to have been. People used to say things that weren't so nice about her, and then she married Zeke before she even graduated. That shut the gossips up, because everybody liked Zeke, you know. Anyway, why I'm telling you this is, it's likely your mama's afraid you're getting too wild and that you'll suffer for it like she did."

Shari made a sound somewhere between a laugh and a cry. Mabel was so far off the mark that it was funny. "Thanks for the ride," Shari said and tried to get the door open.

Mabel reached over and opened it for her. "You feeling wobbly still?"

"I'm fine," Shari said automatically. She offered up as much of a smile as she could manage and got out of the car and went around to the back door.

The peanut-butter sandwich she'd made was still on the floor. She picked it up and threw it in the waste-bin. She'd have to eat soon, even though she felt too nauseous now. She needed her strength if she was going to get herself out of the house before Charlotte got home tonight. She'd deliberately disobeyed her mother, not once, but several times. What would Charlotte do to her? A flash of memory brought back that hand with the long enamelled fingernails as it lifted the screen up on Shari's window. She'd been in the tree outside, and her mother's hand at her window had puzzled her until Shari saw Chirpy fly out. She'd scrambled from her tree and chased him into the woods, calling, but he wouldn't come back, and

Charlotte would never admit it was her fault. Charlotte didn't even remember what she'd done. And Zeke loved Charlotte. Did he love Charlotte's child too, or had he just been kind all these years, pretending to be Shari's father? Unless Charlotte had kept her secret even from him.

Eight

Her heaviness as she climbed through the ravine did not come from the cage she carried with Blue Boy inside clinging to the bars by claws and beak and flapping his wings for balance. The heaviness wasn't even her worry about Peter, but something deeper. Shari concentrated on boxing it away in the furthest recesses of her mind where it couldn't hurt her. She did the trick that usually worked. She concentrated hard on some immediate task, in this case figuring out how to persuade Mrs. Wallace to keep Blue Boy for her. Even if that bird-loving lady were willing, she would want to know why Shari needed the favour. Shari poked around her mind for an excuse, but still had no words ready when she knocked on Mrs. Wallace's door.

"Come in, Mabel," Mrs. Wallace called.

"No, it's me," Shari said and hesitated on the threshold. She saw Mrs. Wallace standing at the oven. A delicious smell of baking bread filled the airy kitchen. Breakfast dishes were draining in a wooden rack, and a ruby-red vase on the windowsill had caught a sunbeam.

"Shari! You came just in time. When I got the urge to bake this dill bread, I hoped somebody would come by and share it with me." Mrs. Wallace stood up and set the steaming loaf she was holding by two oven mitts on a hot pad on the table.

"Come sit down," Mrs. Wallace said. "Why do you have your bird with you?" And then, as she focused on Shari more closely, she asked, "What's wrong?" Her grey eyes narrowed with concern. "What happened to you?"

"Nothing," Shari said. "Would you be willing to take care of Blue Boy for me for a while?"

"Take care of him? Are you going somewhere?"

"Well . . . I don't know. But my little brother's in the hospital, and if . . . I just don't have time to take care of Blue Boy right now, and I thought —"

"Shari, who hit you?"

Shari shook her hair forward and bent her head to hide her face. "Nobody," she said. "It just happened. It isn't anything."

"Isn't it?" Mrs. Wallace lifted Shari's chin and studied her cheek, then gently probed the lump on Shari's head. "This needs to be seen to. Sit here, and while we're waiting for the bread to cool, I'll practise my first aid on you." Her calmness put Shari at ease.

"I took a course," Mrs. Wallace continued. "Figured living up on the mountain by myself, I should know a thing or two about cuts and bruises." She kept talking from the other room and returned quickly with a first-aid box and towels. Shari let her work on the tender place on her head.

"Am I hurting you?" Mrs. Wallace asked as she washed away the dried blood from around the lump with warm, soapy water.

"No," Shari said.

"You're a stoic."

"What that?"

"It's a person who stands up to pain well and doesn't mind hardship. Comes from people who lived in ancient Greece. They were known for being able to take hard knocks without complaining. . . . Why did your mother hit you?"

"She didn't."

"I heard about what happened to your little brother. Mabel called me this morning. Did he fall while you were with me yesterday?"

"Yes. He must have changed his mind and come after me, but he couldn't make it over the ledge alone, so he fell." Shari said. She heard her voice go high on the last words.

"Well, you couldn't help that."

"I'm supposed to watch out for him."

"Every minute of the day?"

Shari hunched her shoulders.

"Your mother is responsible for Peter except when you're with him alone."

To her own astonishment, Shari burst out, "But she hates me. She says it's my fault. And now she won't even let me go to see him. Mabel says he's all right, but he looked like he was dead when I found him yesterday."

"And you ran home and told your mother, and she blamed you. Is that it?" Mrs. Wallace didn't wait for an answer. She insisted, "You can't help what your brother does when you're not with him."

"I told him he could do it. I said he was as good a climber as me, but he's not, and he fell." Shari shuddered. Now her head ached horribly.

"What I don't understand," Mrs. Wallace said, "is what all this has to do with your parakeet."

"Because my mother's mad at me."

Mrs. Wallace whistled softly. "I see," she said. They both heard a car crunching on the gravel drive. "I invited Mabel up for lunch today. You stay too, Shari. I've got homemade blackberry preserves and some good cheese and tomatoes to go with the dill bread."

"Thank you, but—" Shari began her exercise in polite refusal, but Mrs. Wallace interrupted her.

"Stay. I'll take care of Blue Boy as long as you need, but I'll expect you to come visit him often. All right?"

"Yes, thank you," Shari said. She felt so weak, and it felt good just to sit there in the pleasant kitchen and be cared for and fed.

"Well, look who's here!" Mabel said.

"Take a load off your feet, Mabel," Mrs. Wallace said. "Shari's joining our lunch party today."

"Now, isn't that nifty. I see you've been doctoring her some."

"I'm thinking of paying a visit to Shari's mother tomorrow," Mrs. Wallace announced.

"Don't do that," Mabel said. "Hereabouts that'd be considered nosing around in other people's business."

"Some things require interference."

"Nosy neighbours are not appreciated in this part of

the country, Eve. I'm warning you."

"All I'm going to do is pay a social call on Shari's mother."

"You've lived up here—how many years—and you've never seen fit to call on Charlotte Lally before. What are you going to say that you come about?"

"Shari wants me to take care of her bird for her. I'll get her mother's permission. How's that Mabel? Also I can inquire after my friend, Peter."

"Makes no difference to me, as long as you don't go busting in there telling her how to bring up her children. You know, lots of folks don't see nothing wrong in a smack to keep a kid from getting out of hand. Don't you go making a federal case out of nothing."

"What makes you think I'd do that?"

"That look in your eye," Mabel said. "I've known you long enough to recognize when you got your back up."

"Tell me, Mabel, if you saw a parent beating up her child in front of your store, would you sit and watch or jump up and try to stop her?"

"Shari's parents don't beat her up." Mabel sounded horrified. She turned towards Shari. "Do they?"

"No," Shari said, denying what she had always denied even to herself.

"Then what's that hand-shaped bruise on her cheek and the bump on her head from?" Mrs. Wallace asked.

"Shari?" Mabel demanded support in setting Mrs. Wallace straight.

"It's nothing," Shari said. She was protecting not just Charlotte from shame, but her brothers and father and herself as well. Deep down inside her was the guilty sense that she had to be the cause of the wrong that was done her.

"There, you see?" Mabel said to Mrs. Wallace. "This child comes from a perfectly good family. I've known her mother all her life. She's not a bad woman. Maybe Charlotte's grandparents was stricter than they should've been and kept her at home and protected her overmuch. Then she got herself a husband who did the same, until he decided to go off on the road and leave her in charge of four growing kids, which is more than her nerves can stand—"

"Then good neighbours should offer to relieve her when it becomes too much for her nerves," Mrs. Wallace said briskly.

"So long as you don't come right out and accuse Charlotte of nothing," Mabel said. "It wouldn't do Shari no good either, you know. Where's she going to go that's better than her own home?"

"Here if she likes."

Mabel was silenced by the answer. Shari looked at Mrs. Wallace in a daze. "I could come here to stay?" she asked.

"Why not?" Mrs. Wallace said firmly. "I have those two empty beds up in the attic that my granddaughters seldom use. Plenty of space and time." She smiled. "That would be one way to ensure your help in the bird-banding project, Shari."

"Oh, Mrs. Wallace!"

"There," Mrs. Wallace said comfortingly as Shari hid her face in her hands. "There, there. It's just an offer, something you can think about anyway. Meanwhile, let's eat lunch."

Shari went to the bathroom to recover her composure. When she'd washed her hands and returned, Mrs. Wallace and Mabel were talking about the problem of setting up the large nylon-mesh nets to catch the migratory birds without hurting them, so they could be banded and set free.

"They're just like square sails, I believe, and the birds fly into them and tangle their feet and make a pouch in the mesh. Then you've got to go around several times a day to free them. 'Course clipping the little metal band on only takes a few seconds, and after you release them, you make a record of it. I've seen it done, but I've never tried it myself," Mrs. Wallace was saying.

Shari ate some of the crusty, tender dill bread. It tasted better than anything she could remember. She had a second slice and then a third. The warmth in the kitchen from the oven and the fuzziness in her head began to make her very sleepy.

"You lie down and take a nap on my bed," the observant Mrs. Wallace said. She guided Shari into a room with lilac-coloured walls and a lilac print bedspread. Beside the bed were shelves of interesting objects—a painted lace-edged fan, a china ballerina, shells bigger than the biggest pinecones, a fat, funny bowling-pin-shaped doll, a silver coach. The crystal bird was there too.

"May I hold it?" Shari pointed, as Mrs. Wallace threw a rose-and-grey knitted afghan over her.

"Of course." Mrs. Wallace put the bird in her hands. 'It's yours for as long as you need it." She left the room.

Shari closed her eyes gratefully. Before she awoke, she dreamed that she was standing at the end of Peter's hospital bed looking over a rolling bed tray at her little brother's pale, round face.

"Are you really all right?" she asked him.

"Shari? Where were you? I missed you."

"I'm here now. You know I'd be with you if I could, Petey Pie."

"Hug me, Shari," Peter said, and she did, reassured by the solid feel of him in her arms that he was going to be well soon.

She came out of Mrs. Wallace's bedroom feeling renewed. Mabel was just leaving and offered Shari a lift home.

"Yes, thank you," Shari said. Then she hesitated. She wanted to let Mrs. Wallace know how grateful she was for all the kindnesses of the afternoon, and most of all for the promise of a refuge. Just saying thank you wasn't enough. So Shari did the only thing that came to her. She put her arms shyly around Mrs. Wallace's stocky form and hugged her.

"There, there," Mrs. Wallace said, looking pleased and patting Shari's back. "If you need me, just call."

"Did you really mean that I could take the crystal bird with me?" Shari asked.

"That's what I mean," Mrs. Wallace said. "And I mean what I said about living here too." She wrapped the bird in a paper towel, and Shari carried it off in her hand. It was precious now, not only because of its beauty, but because it was proof of Mrs. Wallace's belief in her.

Nine

Charlotte was in a good mood at supper that night. As she served them a salad of cold tuna fish and mixed vegetables with mayonnaise, she told them, "The doctor says Peter could've been crippled or brain damaged from that fall, but likely he won't be. No thanks to you, Miss Shari Ape Face. Where'd you spend the day? Out in the woods again?"

"I took Blue Boy over to Mrs. Wallace's and left him there."

"What for?" The sharp edge of Charlotte's voice jabbed Doug into attention, and even Walter looked up from the book he was reading at the table.

"I don't feel like taking care of Blue Boy right now, not until Pete is well," Shari said and added, "Mrs. Wallace may come by to see you. She wants to ask if it's all right if she keeps my bird."

"You crazy? What do I care what she does with it? Make her pay for the cage though if she ends up keeping him for good." Charlotte looked at her suspiciously. "Did you tell her anything?"

"About what?"

"About how much you hate your mother, or anything

like that."

"I don't tell things," Shari said. "Anyway, you're the one who hates me." As soon as the words left her mouth, Shari stood up and backed away from the table, afraid that she'd triggered an explosion.

"Sit down," Charlotte said. "I'm not going to hit you. I only got mad at you because you let Peter hurt himself. Don't start pretending to be scared of me all of a sudden. You've never been scared of me in your life."

"I don't like getting hit," Shari said.

"I didn't hit you. A slap once in a while isn't hitting. And *you* don't feel it anyway. Don't feel nothing, never did. Even when you were tiny, you didn't cry. I used to wonder if you were human, the way nothing seemed to hurt you."

"She cries," Walter said quickly. "I've seen her."

"You have?" Charlotte glanced at him and away. "Well, you've seen more than me then," she said bitterly and began to clear away the dishes.

Shari hadn't finished eating, but she took her plate to the sink anyway.

"I got invited to go fishing tomorrow," Doug said. "You want to take my place at the stand with Walter, Shari?"

"Okay," she agreed, pleased he would trust her.

"We'll pay you a percentage of whatever we make. Not a lot. Say ten per cent, maybe twenty depending on how good a day it is."

"That's okay." Shari would have offered to do it for nothing, but she thought she could use the money to

121

bring Peter something nice. "Whatever you want to give me would be fine."

Alone in her room, she stood idly thinking that tomorrow would be a pleasant day in the shade of the tree where the boys had set up their vegetable stand. Walter would read in between customers while she watched the cars go by and gave change and bagged the corn and tomatoes people bought. Hours would pass quickly, bringing her another day closer to when Peter would come home and another day closer to when Zeke would return. She had something to ask Zeke, and if his answer told her that she had been mistaking kindness for love, then her whole life was going to change.

She knelt on her bed at the window listening to the lulling night sounds—the cry of a hunting bird, the peep and buzz of insects, the swish of passing cars—all interwoven with the whisper of the wind through the leaves. But the web of sound failed to soothe her as it usually did. An ache was swelling in her chest, expanding so fast she was afraid she couldn't contain it. It came from the words Charlotte had spoken. It dealt with who Shari was, and she feared that if she recognized it, she would become another person, someone without anyone at all to love.

Walter and Shari straggled in from their day at the vegetable stand to find Charlotte lying on a folding metal lounge chair in the drive, smoking and reading one of the movie magazines she regularly borrowed from BeeJay's shop.

"Your friend stopped by," Charlotte said to Shari.

"She seems quite taken with you. Brought me some kind of bread she made. She said you and her have a lot in common, the way you like birds and all. I told her it was all right with me if she wants to keep your parakeet at her place."

"Good," Shari said, relieved that Mrs. Wallace's visit hadn't made Charlotte angry.

"She invited me to come by her house," Charlotte continued. "I told her that dirt road of hers was too much for me to drive with my old banger. I don't have no four-wheel-drive pickup like she's got. . . . Guess she likes being alone up there."

"She doesn't mind being alone," Shari agreed.

"Like you. Looks like you're a pair, you and that weird old lady."

"She's not weird," Shari said.

"Well, just don't hang around her too much or you'll wear out your welcome."

"I won't wear it out." A breathlessness overtook Shari, and then she lashed out at Charlotte with a boast. "Mrs. Wallace said I could come and live with her if I want."

"She said that in so many words?"

"Yes."

"And you'd go?"

"I might."

"Just what I'd expect from you. Pick up and leave us just like that!" Charlotte illustrated with a snap of her fingers. "Like your own family don't mean a thing to you."

"Shari," Walter said, "aren't you going to wait till Pete

gets out of the hospital?"

"I don't know," Shari said feeling powerful.

Charlotte's eyes were filled with tears as she teetered between being hurt and being furious. The fury won. "Don't you dare go to that woman. We're your family here. We're your family and you belong with us."

"But I don't," Shari said. "You told me yourself I don't belong to anybody here except you, and *you* hate me." She was flying, flying over the abyss, amazed at her own recklessness.

"Run, Shari," Walter yelled. He left the carport and the unsold food they'd brought back and stepped towards her, then stopped. She saw Charlotte rising from her lounge chair, saw her lunge, hand raised to strike.

Instinctively, Shari dashed towards the woods. She thought of heading for Mrs. Wallace's house, but realized that was the first place Charlotte would check. Up the mountain then. Shari zigzagged through the trees towards Eagle's Perch. Why had she let the words fly out of her like that? She'd been guarding her tongue all her life, but lately it seemed whenever she opened her mouth, words flew out—to Mrs. Wallace, to Charlotte, whose anger was so easily roused. Shari couldn't understand what had got into her. Her ability to control herself had always been her greatest protection.

On the ledge near the narrow peak of the mountain, hours later, she watched the shadows sweep across the valley floor. The pale evening sky turned up a single star. The darkness rose up from the earth and spread heavenward. As the knowledge she had tried to hide from crept up on her, she wished she had some charm to give her courage. Even the crystal bird would have helped. But it was in her room, hidden in her boot. Zeke was not her father. But what was even worse—Peter was not really her brother. Her only real relative was Charlotte. Shari mourned the family she had lost. Hour after hour, she mourned, hour after hour until the pain burned itself out and even the ashes were cooling.

At last she began to feel her way back down in the moonlight to the only place she could go to escape her mother's wrath. She walked in open spaces now because it was too dark to see beneath the trees. By midnight, she was knocking on Mrs. Wallace's door.

Mrs. Wallace opened the door, wearing a nightgown under a plaid flannel robe. Her face was as fresh and firm and her white hair as neat as during the day. "What are you doing roaming around in the middle of the night, Shari?" she asked.

"I saw your light. I thought you might be awake."

"So I am. Come on in. I've been reading a dull book about railroads. Dull books either put me to sleep or teach me enough to make being awake worthwhile. Try it sometime if you have trouble sleeping."

Without asking Shari whether she was hungry or not, Mrs. Wallace sat her down at the kitchen table and started putting food in front of her. "Pick at that chicken while I heat up this milk for hot chocolate. Or would you prefer it cold?"

"However you like it," Shari said.

"Hot then.... The police came by this evening." Mrs.

Wallace glanced at Shari as she spoke. "Seems your mother sent them. I expect we'd better call and tell her you're all right."

"You said yesterday I could live with you. Did you mean it?" Shari asked.

"Yes. You realize it will only work if your folks agree to allow it. Otherwise we'd have to go to court, and that could be a long and messy business."

Instead of considering that problem, Shari thought of Peter. He'd come home from the hospital and he'd miss her if she wasn't there. Even if he wasn't her real brother, he would miss her. Of course, she could spend time with him still—unless Charlotte wouldn't let him see her anymore. "My mother got angry when I told her you said I could live with you."

"I know," Mrs. Wallace said dryly. "She gave me what for over the phone for trying to steal your affections."

"I don't know why she cares, because she doesn't care about me," Shari said.

"Do you want to wait until your father comes home and talk it over with him?" Mrs. Wallace asked.

"I don't have a father," Shari said.

Mrs. Wallace poured Shari's hot chocolate into a mug and brought it to her, then filled a mug for herself. Finally, she sat down and said, "That's some statement." A moth flew crazily at the light of the umbrella-shaped lamp hanging over them. "Did your mother tell you that—that you don't have a father?"

"Yes."

"And that's why you ran away tonight?"

"Not exactly. Except I guess what happened tonight was because it made me so mad that—I don't know. It's awful to find out you're not who you thought. All my life I thought Zeke was my father."

"And you were glad of that?"

"Oh, yes. Zeke's wonderful. He's good to me. Only, he loves my mother best, of course."

"You're hurting, Shari. I can see it."

"Yes, I hurt," Shari admitted, "worse than anything."

"Did Charlotte tell you who your natural father is?"

"No. I didn't think to ask. She didn't like him much—after. She said he left her when—" Shari's voice trailed off, silenced by the old habit of not telling private family business.

"Maybe your mother didn't like him just because he left her. It's possible you might have a perfectly nice father somewhere, Shari."

Shari shook her head. "I don't care. Even if Zeke isn't my father, I don't need anybody else besides him."

"I'd tell him that if I were you."

"Tell him?"

"That you love him. Sure. Chances are he loves you as much as you do him."

"Do you think he knows he's not my real father?"

"What do you think?"

Shari considered. "I could ask him when he comes back. Then—if you wouldn't mind, I'll come and live with you, Mrs. Wallace."

"Mind?" Mrs. Wallace said. "It would be a treat for me. You're close to the age of my grandchildren, just between the youngest and the oldest. It would be like having a third granddaughter around."

The statement touched Shari, and she didn't know what to say, but Mrs. Wallace understood without words. She patted Shari's hand. "Why don't you go and see Blue Boy while I call your mother to tell her you're safe."

"I'd rather you called the police and let them tell her," Shari said.

"Just as you please," Mrs. Wallace said.

When Mrs. Wallace reached the sheriff's office, she was told to keep Shari where she was. The sheriff would come for her. Mrs. Wallace hung up and said, "I guess you have to go home tonight whether I want you to or not."

Shari looked unhappy.

"You know," Mrs. Wallace said, "my good friend Mabel believes that every mother loves her child and that it's a child's duty to love her back. Do you think Mabel's right?"

"I don't know." It was the kind of subject Shari avoided thinking about. She looked at Mrs. Wallace, who was patiently waiting for an answer. For her sake, Shari tried. "Sometimes you just can't love somebody. And I guess some children aren't very lovable. I guess . . . I don't know."

"Well, I do," Mrs. Wallace said. "I've seen mothers who don't love their children and some who seem to pick on one particular child in a mean way. It can also happen that a mother doesn't have much love in her to give. And sometimes a mother and child don't fit well together and get on each other's nerves. It's not that the child is bad, or even that the mother is, it's just that they can't get along well living together. It's remarkable how little most families are like our ideal of how they should be."

"I hate my mother," Shari said in a husky voice. "Sometimes I really hate her." She held her breath in surprise at what she had said. She had never let the thought surface before, never opened that particular box. The closest she had ever come was thinking that Charlotte was the one doing the hating.

If Mrs. Wallace was shocked, she didn't show it. All she said was, "When you're older and on your own, you may understand your mother better and forgive her."

"I won't forgive her," Shari said. "She took Zeke and Peter away from me."

"Shari, she couldn't do that. She doesn't have the power. You'll see." Mrs. Wallace took her hand and squeezed it.

Shari didn't argue, but this time she knew Mrs. Wallace was wrong.

When the sheriff arrived, red-eyed and tired looking, Mrs. Wallace was showing Shari the guest beds up in the attic where her grandchildren usually slept. Mrs. Wallace offered the sheriff a cup of coffee, but he refused politely and said to Shari, "Let's get cracking, girl. Your poor mother's not going to sleep until she gets her baby girl home safe and sound."

"I hope her poor mother has her temper under control tonight," Mrs. Wallace said coolly and tipped Shari's chin up towards the light so that the sheriff could see her cheek. Shari had forgotten that Charlotte's hand was imprinted there in purple.

"I see," he said. "Well, if there's any trouble, I'll expect someone to report it."

"I'll report it if I hear about it," Mrs. Wallace said.

"You got any problem with going home now, young lady?" the sheriff asked, bending his wavy grey hair and veiny nose towards Shari so he could watch her expression as she answered him.

"I'll be okay," she said.

"She's a spunky girl," Mrs. Wallace informed the sheriff.

"All right, all right. I'll let the woman know her child's got friends. That's all it takes usually, just a hint or two."

"Tomorrow morning," Mrs. Wallace said to Shari, "I'll just stop by your house for a minute and see how you're doing. Okay?"

"Give Blue Boy a kiss for me when he wakes up," Shari told Mrs. Wallace.

Shari stepped out of the sheriff's car to find Charlotte waiting for her with open arms. It was the first hug her mother had given her in years.

"Guess everything is all right here for now. You call if you need me again," the sheriff said as he left. It wasn't clear whether he was talking to Shari or Charlotte.

"Zeke called in tonight, and I told him you were gone and to get home fast," Charlotte said breathlessly. "He's going to deliver the load he's got now and be back here by tomorrow night, but before that, you and me got some talking to do."

Alone in her room, Shari reached into her boot and withdrew the crystal bird. She could live so peacefully with Mrs. Wallace, but what if that meant living without Peter? It would become difficult to see him, and when she saw him, suppose they had become strangers to one another. Her longing to see him at that very moment was immense. She was so afraid of losing him again. The first time had been in the ravine when she thought that he was dead. This time it would be by her own choice. It was clear to her that she needed Peter more than he needed her. He had a family, but she was only his half sister and Doug and Walter's half sister and no blood relation to Zeke at all. She had nobody. Her whole life she had believed herself to be part of a family and half of a loving pair, but all she had now was Charlotte. She grasped the crystal bird tightly, trying to squeeze comfort from its smooth weight, but nothing eased the agony, not even the tears that finally came.

Charlotte's touch on her shoulder made Shari open her eyes. "You overslept. It's nearly noon. You never slept this late before. Tired yourself out with all your running yesterday, didn't you?"

Cautiously, Shari looked at her mother. Charlotte was bright faced and eager looking, girlish in jeans and tight green tee shirt that matched her eyes.

"Zeke's coming," Shari said, remembering.

"Should be here by supper time. Thanks to you and your shenanigans. What'd you run away for like that?'

Shari could detect no anger in her mother's voice.

Probably Charlotte was glad of an excuse to get Zeke back early.

"Was it true what you told me, that he's not my father?" Shari dared to ask, at the same time automatically drawing back to the far corner of her bed and pulling her knees protectively against her chest.

"You want to hear about it?" Charlotte sounded curiously friendly. Without waiting for Shari's answer, she settled onto the bed and drew her knees up, clasping her hands around them in a mirror image of Shari's posture. "I was just a high-school kid," Charlotte began. "I was pretty and all the boys were after me, but your father was the one I wanted. Don't ask me why. He never had much to say for himself, and he was only a wiry little fellow, no handsome football type, let me tell you. He gave flying lessons at the airport, and he was a lot older than me, but I went with him. . . . He left me when I told him I was pregnant. Picked up and ran off even though he was twenty-five and I was only a kid. He didn't love me at all like he said." Her voice tightened. "What he loved was flying. Later on, I heard on the news that he got killed skydiving. I used to have dreams watching him fall from the sky. Not that it bothered me. He didn't care about me. Why should I feel bad about him? Anyways, instead of going into fashion like I'd wanted, I married Zeke and had you and that's what I got your father to thank for."

"So he's dead."

"Yes, but don't waste time grieving about that. He wasn't much, believe me."

"Did you love Zeke?"

"When I married him? Not then. He was just an older guy who'd always been sweet on me. I used to get him to drive me out to the airport sometimes, and he'd give me a hard time about cutting school. Not that the school ever knew. They had my timetable so messed up that I could leave after homeroom, and my teachers never did figure out where I was supposed to be. If my grandparents had known, they'd have killed me."

Shari didn't stir, and Charlotte went on talking. "They wanted to kill poor Zeke when we eloped because they thought he was the one. If he'd have given me the money to have an abortion like I wanted instead of marrying me, it would've worked out better." Charlotte's face creased with pain. "My grandparents were so mad at me! They packed up and moved to Florida and didn't write or call until after Walter was born. Then they wanted me to come down for a visit, but how could I with three little kids? And it got them that I never finished high school. I never did get up the courage to tell them it wasn't Zeke's fault I got pregnant. Nobody knew that, just Zeke and me."

"Were your grandparents nice?" Shari asked, feeling a sympathy for her mother that she'd never experienced before.

"Well, they weren't easy." Charlotte's voice sharpened. "They wouldn't have suited *you*, the way you like to run around as you please. They raised me good and proper."

"And you loved them?"

"Sure I did. . . . Well, anyways, they left me their

money when they died, and that's how we come to buy this house. It was their money we used. Of course, I wanted to buy a place in the city instead, but Zeke wouldn't move away from here." A long sigh escaped her.

"I told you Mrs. Wallace says I can live with her," Shari said.

"So?"

"So I might go."

"You *would* want to do something like that. You would go and disgrace us by moving in with a stranger like we don't provide for you good."

"I'm not trying to disgrace you. It's just—"

"Oh, don't do me any favours. My friends'll know the truth. I try hard to be a good mother even though I get sick to death of it. Nobody sees *me* running around the bars at night like some women whose husbands are gone all the time. *You're* the one's going to look bad if you move out of here, not me."

"I don't care what people think," Shari said quietly.

"No, that's one of your big problems. You don't care about anyone but yourself."

"That's not true," Shari said as Charlotte rose and started out of the room.

"Who do you care about then?" Charlotte asked. Her face was flushed as she looked back over her shoulder at Shari.

"Peter and Zeke. And Mrs. Wallace."

"There's someone else should mean more to you," Charlotte said bitterly and jerked the door shut behind her.

The crystal bird dug into Shari's elbow when she sat up. She pressed its coolness to her cheek, then tucked the bird back into the boot and got dressed thinking about Charlotte's revelations. That her father had been a pilot struck Shari as a sign. He had given her something whether he had wanted to or not, his agility and his yearning to sail weightlessly across the sky. She had been born to be a flyer, and she would not let anyone stop her from becoming one. She would not be like her mother who'd been frustrated all her life in everything she'd wanted to do. Charlotte had never got what she wanted, not the husband nor the career, nor even the location to live. If only Charlotte were less spiteful, Shari could pity her. As it was, even understanding her mother's bitterness didn't help Shari to forgive her.

The sudden racket of an angry blue jay in the tree outside Shari's window reminded her of Blue Boy. Living with Mrs. Wallace meant having him back again, but what she still needed to figure out was how to hang on to Peter. If only she could take Peter along with her! Before she made Charlotte angry, she should have asked when Pete was coming home. Charlotte could so easily refuse to let Shari visit him, and he couldn't get through the ravine by himself. He couldn't go the long miles by the highway either, unless someone drove him. She had better talk to Zeke before she made any final decisions.

When Shari came out of the bathroom, she saw Charlotte getting car keys out of her shoulder bag and grabbing a pack of cigarettes from an open carton. "I'm going to the hospital," Charlotte said.

"How is Petey?"

"Okay. Coming along at least."

"Can I go with you?"

"No, you stay here. Peter might as well get used to not having you around since you're moving out on us." Charlotte tossed her head and left.

Shari had an urge to run after her and plead to go along, but she knew it was useless to try. She gripped the counter, listening to the raucous sound of the car's engine revving up and diminishing as Charlotte drove off. The day was full of the promise of rain, moiling clouds overhead and distant thunderclaps. Shari might have run off to the woods anyway, but she had no desire to today.

To keep herself from brooding, she decided to make brownies. Luckily, there was enough unsweetened chocolate for the cookbook recipe Zeke like especially. He might be willing to deliver some to Peter for her. A quake of thunder split the sky, and it got so dark outside that Shari turned on the light in the kitchen. She even switched on the radio, but beside the country-western channel that her mother listened to, all that was on was a talk show with people calling in about teenage drinking. Better to listen to the thunder. Once the brownies were in the oven, the thoughts she'd been avoiding crowded in on her. It didn't help to busy herself cleaning up her own mess and the sink full of dirty dishes from breakfast. The thoughts persisted.

However wary she had been of Charlotte's anger, Charlotte had been "Mother". Charlotte had been unfair and hurtful, but she had still been "Mother", that human security blanket every child needed. Now suddenly such distance had opened between them that Shari was seeing Charlotte as a person outside her parental role, not an especially nice person, with her flaring temper and her weasel way of lying when it suited her needs. She had more meanness in her than other adults had, more hate, and not all of it was directed at Shari either. Charlotte hated anyone who got in her way. Even Peter. She had moments of showering affection on him, but mostly she ignored him and was glad to leave him in his sister's charge so as not to be bothered with him. And Doug and Walter—Charlotte liked them well enough when they were out of the house. She gave them credit for earning money and digging out the drive in winter and mowing the lawn in summer, but when their squabbling or horsing around bothered her, she would lash out at them too, scream at them to shut up and get out of her sight.

What Charlotte liked best was to sit talking about how hard she had it over a cup of coffee with BeeJay. But when BeeJay went home, Charlotte would make remarks about her, about why BeeJay had been divorced three times and how she was a lot older than she admitted to being. There was no one to whom Charlotte was loyal, unless it was Zeke. The disappointments of her life were sad, and having three babies before she was twenty probably had been hard for Charlotte, but not hard enough so that Shari could excuse her mother's lack of human kindness.

Shari listened to the rush of water in the sink as she scrubbed the pot with the burned-on baked beans that had been left to soak overnight. If only the problem were simply that Charlotte hadn't wanted a child—any child. It would be hard to know she hadn't been wanted, but Shari could deal with that. What bothered her more was the feeling that it as her own fault that her mother didn't love her. Mrs. Wallace had said that Shari wasn't to blame. What a relief to believe that she wasn't the unloving creature Charlotte accused her of being.

Shari stood at the doorway watching the translucent streamers of rain making the earth into a batter as dark as the baking brownies. Rain drummed on the roof, slapped the window-panes, and hissed in the leaves. The heavy green scent of summer competed with the odour of warm chocolate in the kitchen.

The front door slammed as Charlotte dashed into the house. Shari heard Walter and Doug's voices. Charlotte must have picked them up at their stand on her way home.

"Stack all that stuff in the carport and come in the back way with your muddy feet," Charlotte told them. She herself walked into the kitchen. Her eyes went to the sink. "I see you decided to do something useful for a change," she said.

"I do a lot of things that are useful," Shari said. "I take care of Peter all the time."

Charlotte frowned. "What's got into you? I'm not telling you you did anything wrong. . . . Here," she said. "I went shopping at the mall after I stopped by to see Peter, and I bought you a new pair of jeans. The ones you got are falling into holes. Here . . ." She rattled a thin paper bag, one of several she was holding. "See if they fit."

"Why didn't you ever tell me before that I wasn't Zeke's child?" Shari asked, taking the bag, but not looking into it as the question that had been at the back of her mind shot out of her mouth.

"You still chewing that over? All right, if you must know, I promised Zeke that I'd never tell you, and if you hadn't made me so mad—"

"Will Zeke be angry if I tell him I know?"

Charlotte slapped the packages onto the kitchen table and squared off for a fight. "You threatening me? Think I care what you tell him? Zeke'd never hold anything against me for long. He's still crazy about me, for your information, Miss Shari Ape Face."

"I wasn't threatening you, just asking," Shari said. "Because I need to talk to Zeke."

"Why?"

"To find out—" She had trouble putting her need into words. "About where I am." She looked at her mother calmly. Never before in her life had she felt as free of Charlotte. If it wasn't Shari's fault, if it was just Charlotte's nature to be mean, then Shari owed her mother nothing. No need to fear her any more. With nothing due and nothing to expect, the bond between them was broken.

Doug and Walter tramped in the back door, dripping wet. They yanked off their muddy trainers and dropped them on the mat beside the door.

"Boy, today was the worst!" Doug complained, heading for the towel rack. "Nobody hardly stopped by the stand. Tomorrow, we're going to stay home and do something that's fun for a change."

"Ma, tomorrow, could you drive me by the library?" Walter asked. "I got four overdue books."

"Don't bother me now," Charlotte said as she opened the refrigerator. "Your father's going to walk in any minute, and I haven't figured out what to make for supper yet."

"Is he gonna leave again right away when he finds out Shari got home all right?" Walter asked.

"How should I know? Anyway, she's not planning to stay around for long. Wonder what he's going to say about *that* when he gets here," Charlotte gave Shari a resentful glance and smacked a pot down on the stove.

"Where are you going, Shari?" Doug asked.

"I might go and live with Mrs. Wallace," Shari said. "But I don't know for sure yet."

"What do you want to go and do that for?" Doug asked with a puzzled frown on his meaty face.

Shari shrugged. "Just because," she said. She felt Walter looking at her, all big ears and thinking eyes.

"Can one of us move into Shari's room then? Can I?" Doug asked Charlotte.

"Don't bother me about it. Ask your father."

Walter pulled a paperback out of his jeans' pocket and sat down at the kitchen table to read. Shari felt bad seeing him curl up into his book with nothing to say to her. He was her brother, after all. Then she remembered—no, he wasn't.

Ten

Zeke didn't get home until after Shari had gone to bed that night, but she found him sitting at the kitchen table working on his accounts the next morning. Nobody else was up yet. She was so glad to see him there and to have him to herself for once that she threw her arms around his back and hugged him uninvited. When she remembered he wasn't her real father anymore, she let go and took a step back in a sudden fit of shyness.

"What's up, Shari honey? You been having a hard time lately?" He hugged her around in front of him and kissed her, then offered her a knee to perch on. She sat on the chair across from him instead and leaned her elbows on the table.

"Zeke, is Peter getting out of the hospital soon?"

"Didn't your mother tell you? We're picking him up today."

"Oh, good! Can I go with you?"

"Sure." He sipped from his coffee mug, studying her. "Every time I come home, even if I've only been gone a day, you look more grown up and prettier."

"I'm not pretty," Shari said.

"Sure you are. Pretty as a chipmunk. You're small-boned and neat and quick."

Shari smiled. "Thanks a lot," she mocked his compliment.

"You don't think chipmunks are pretty?"

She shrugged. His broad face half covered with a stubble of on-the-road beard was so dear to her, but she made herself say, "I need to talk to you about something important, Zeke."

"I figured you might. Charlotte said she let slip about your dad."

Shari nodded, heat rising to her cheeks. It was painful to talk to the man whom she loved as a father, who wasn't her father, about the stranger who was. It didn't surprise her to hear that Charlotte had already confessed. Just the tactics she would use. Tell first so that Shari couldn't hold anything over her. Not that Shari would have, but Charlotte didn't have a high enough regard for her to know that.

"It's a pretty morning after all that rain," Zeke said. "Want to walk down the road for a bit?"

"Yes." She was grateful for the offer.

"Tell you what," he said. "Why don't we go to the ravine where Peter had his accident. I ought to look that place over anyhow."

"It wasn't my fault," Shari thought to tell Zeke. "He said he wanted to stay home, and Mother was here, so I went to see my friend, Mrs. Wallace, and then he decided to follow me."

"I know how you love him, honey. And you take good care of him too. No way did I ever think it was your fault," Zeke assured her.

Outside, a million glittering dewdrops clung to every grass blade and leaf. The air smelled of rich earth and tangy pines, better to Shari than any perfume Zeke had ever bought Charlotte. They walked together through woods so canopied with leaves that the undergrowth was sparse and the ground felt springy from evergreen needles and autumns of dead oak and beech and birch and hickory leaves.

"Well, then," Zeke said when she didn't begin talking to him. "How about it? Now you know I'm not your blood father, do you still love me?"

"Me?" she asked, indignant that he could ask such a question as if she were the one to change. "I love you just as much as ever. You're who you always were. Except—"

"There is no except, Shari." He took her by the shoulders and turned her around to face him. "You're who you always were to me too. You were my little girl from the day you were born. First time you looked up at me and smiled, I loved you and I've never stopped. People ask me how many kids I've got and I say four and never think that you're any different from your brothers. Although, being a girl does make you special. Don't tell on me to your brothers, but I'm partial to little girls." The grin made his face knobbly and brought out the lines around his eyes, which were beaming warmly down on her.

She squeezed his hand.

"Maybe it's a good thing Charlotte told you, though I never wanted her to. I don't know," Zeke said. "She just never got over what he did to her."

"My father?"

"The man that put his seed in her and left her. *I'm* your father," Zeke said forcefully. "I'm the one who raised you and don't you forget it."

"I won't. But Zeke, what was he like? You knew him, didn't you?"

"Yeah, he liked planes. Liked to show off too, always ready to take a dare. How he died was he tried to break the free-fall record and he went too long without opening his chute. When Charlotte saw in the newspaper that he'd killed himself, that was when she stopped hoping he'd come back for her and said she'd marry me. I guess I owe him something for that. Lord knows how long she would've waited if he hadn't killed himself. She sure had it bad for that fella."

"But she loves you so much—"

"Well, *now* she does. But at first I was the one did all the loving. It wasn't until after you was born that she changed. But even before she did, I considered myself a lucky fella. She was the prettiest girl in the valley and lovable, a fun-loving girl. And she had an idea about going away to New York or some big city. I guess she wanted to work for a fancy department store or something like that. The way I see it, if she hadn't fallen for that stunt man, she never would've married me. Isn't it something the way life works out, Shari?"

"Yes," she agreed. In her mind she saw him falling, a thin wiry man, exultant as the air swished by him. His body must have felt light as a bird's, as if the air were cushioning him and he were strong enough to ride the currents and dip and swoop and soar like a hawk, like an eagle, free of all but the flying. He must have been thrilled in those moments of risk and supremely happy the day he died.

"It kind of shook me when you asked me about becoming a pilot," Zeke said. "Remember? I told you not to say that to your mother. Now you understand why. I never would've thought something like that could be inherited."

"It could be accidental," she said. "Or flying might be like a talent, like musical ability that you can inherit."

"Well, it's a mystery to me," Zeke said. "But I don't care what you inherited from him, so long as we got it straight who's your father."

"You are," she said happily.

"That's right." He grinned and gave her an extra squeeze. "And mighty proud of it too."

Zeke was horrified when he saw the ledge on the far side of the ravine. "You climbed over that by yourself? You climbed over that and hoisted your little brother over with you?"

Zeke was so incredulous that she said, "It's not that hard. Watch, I'll show you." Surefooted, she ran across the log and then from toehold to toehold, past bush and rock until she reached the overhanging ledge. Despite his cry of alarm, she lifted herself quickly over and stood up at the top.

"Get back down here," he said. "You're scaring the pants off me."

"It's not as steep as it looks from the bottom," she assured him when she had returned to his side, "and it's the only way I can get to my friend. The road takes too long. It's miles and miles by the road."

"You like her a lot, that lady. How come?" he asked.

"Because," Shari said and shrugged. It would insult him to say that Mrs. Wallace was the first adult who had ever understood her. "I guess because we both like birds and she teaches me stuff. . . . She's nice."

"Your mother says you want to go and live with her."

"Mrs. Wallace said if I wanted to live with her, I could."

"And you want to go?"

"Well, I'd miss you and Petey."

He squeezed her hand and said earnestly, "I'd feel really bad if you left home before you were grown up and ready. That's going to come soon enough." He stroked her hair and ran his fingers down her cheek. "Shari, you and your mother—I know a girl your age sometimes has a hard time getting along with her own mother."

"She hates me?"

"No, she doesn't. She's a nervous woman, emotional, you know? And she does pick on you more than on your brothers, but she doesn't mean nothing by it." He sounded apologetic.

"Don't worry. It's not your fault," Shari said. She knew he couldn't help seeing Charlotte as his sweetheart, the good wife who waited at home for him to return. He loved Charlotte blindly, but then he loved Shari too.

They walked home through the singing woods hand in hand. "What I'm going to do is put a climbing rope down over that ledge so you got something to grip going up it, a good thick rope with knots in it," Zeke said. "But don't you let Peter go up it alone."

"I won't."

"I remember when I was a kid, the places we used to climb and the things we'd try—if our parents knew the half of it, they would've had a fit. But a kid can get hurt easy."

"I know," Shari said.

"And you know how much you and Peter mean to me. Yeah, you know now, don't you?" He hugged her.

She sat in the back seat of the car along with Walter and Doug. They dropped Walter off at the library, and Zeke and Doug went to the hardware store while Shari followed Charlotte up to Peter's room. He looked small sitting on the edge of his bed, already dressed in shorts and a tee shirt and sneakers, ready to leave.

"Shari!" he cried. They met halfway between the door and the bed and wrapped their arms tightly around each other. "Boy, did I miss you," he complained, just as she'd imagined he would. "How come you didn't come visit me?"

"Because I didn't think she should after what she did," Charlotte said when Shari didn't answer. "Listen you two, I got to go down to the desk and fill out all kinds of papers before they let us out of here. Shari, you see to it he packs all his stuff. Zeke's going to take the six of us out to lunch on the way home."

"Wow, can I have a malted and French fries?" Peter

asked.

"Maybe. We'll see," Charlotte said and disappeared.

The other bed in the room was surrounded by white curtains on metal rods. "He's got tubes up his nose," Peter said. "He had an operation yesterday, I think." Then he whispered in Shari's ear, "I think he's going to die."

"No," Shari said. "They'll make him well, Peter. He probably just looks sick because of the operation."

"I hope so," Peter said. "I wouldn't like to die, Shari."

"No. Me neither."

"I'm not going to climb on that hill alone no more."

"That's okay, Pete. I'll go with you."

"Maybe when I get bigger, then I can climb. But I'll never be as good as you."

"Sure you will."

"No, I won't. You're the best climber."

"Well, you're the best talker then."

"Oh yeah, I'm good at that. The nurses call me motor mouth. Did you miss me, Shari?"

"Very much."

"Is Blue Boy talking yet?"

"I don't know. I took him up to Mrs. Wallace's. She's keeping him for me."

"Why?"

"Just because I didn't think he'd be safe at home."

"Isn't it safe at home?"

"I think it's getting safer," she said. "Come on. Let's see what you've got to pack in here." She opened the small suitcase Charlotte had given her and began to put the few items from Peter's bedside closet into it.

*

The happiest days of the summer came next. "Long as I'm home again, might as well make this my vacation," Zeke had said. They went swimming at the lake twice, and one day Zeke took them to a state fair, where Peter was ecstatic because he won a large stuffed bear in a bingo game. Shari rode the tilt-a-whirl three times in a row and was fascinated by the auto thrill show in the stadium.

Shortly before school opened, she started following a body-building programme that Doug had taken up and dropped, and when Peter asked her what she was doing, she said, "Getting in shape to join the air force."

"Now?"

"I have to be ready when I'm old enough."

Peter exercised with her the first day, although he couldn't do a push-up and his sit-ups were elbow-assisted. He was best at running on the spot. Zeke put an early end to the second exercise session by asking for help to hang a climbing rope from a tree over the lip at the top of the ravine. Peter and Shari both volunteered.

"You give Mrs. Wallace an answer to her offer yet?" Zeke asked, as they walked from the car to the tree on the back road above the ravine. He carried the coil of heavy-duty rope already knotted at intervals for easy handholds.

"Not yet," Shari said. "When your vacation is over, I'll go see her then."

"And what are you going to tell her?"

"I don't know."

"It sure would be nice if you'd make up your mind. I bet Mrs. Wallace is wondering too, Shari."

Shari looked at him in surprise. "Why should she be?"

"Well, likely she's lonely and hoping to get your company."

"I don't think so," Shari said. "That's not why she offered me a home. She doesn't mind being alone. I don't either."

He ruffled her hair, smiling. "You're such a funny kid," he said. "Half the time I can't begin to figure what you got in your head. I'll tell the truth. I'm going to feel real bad if you're not home to greet me next time I get off the road."

"Me too," Peter said.

"I won't go unless I have to," was all Shari could tell them.

Charlotte had been easy to get along with while Zeke was home, but even after he left, she kept her black moods to herself and treated Shari with a cautious respect. One morning Shari was doing her exercises in the middle of the living room while Peter kept count for her rather than do the exercises himself.

"What are you doing, training for the Olympics?" Charlotte asked.

"No, just making myself stronger," Shari said.

"What for?"

"In case I want to join the air force some day."

"You really think ahead don't you?" Charlotte said, and then grudgingly, "I wish I had when I was a kid."

"You could do something now," Shari said. "You could get a job or something. I'd watch Peter for you after school."

Charlotte tapped her unlit cigarette against the pack from which she'd just removed it. "I thought you were leaving us."

"If you need me, I could stay. Mrs. Wallace wants me to help her with the bird banding, but I could take Peter with me sometimes for that. It'd work out."

"How come you're so eager for me to get a job?" Charlotte asked.

"I think you'd like being out of the house more."

"Zeke wouldn't like it though if I was."

"He would if he thought it was making you happier."

"I'll think about it," Charlotte said. She started out of the room, stopped and turned around to add, "I forgot to tell you, Mrs. Wallace called and asked how you and Peter are doing."

"I'm going to visit her soon, today maybe."

"What do you want to be friends with an old person like that for anyway?"

"I like her."

"Yeah? I wonder. I wonder if she just don't feel sorry for you because you told her I beat you up and treat you mean."

"I never told her anything like that."

"You didn't? Then how come she offered to let you come and live with her?"

"Because—" Shari stopped exercising, trying to remember how it had been. Had she betrayed Charlotte to Mrs. Wallace? Shari thought guiltily that possibly she had. "I don't usually talk about you to anybody. I was

151

just feeling bad that time because Petey was in the hospital, and you said it was my fault, and I was afraid you'd do something to the bird like you did to Chirpy last summer."

Charlotte gasped. "I never did nothing to your parakeet."

"You opened the window and let him fly out. I saw you."

Charlotte was silent. Her face turned red and she looked as if she were about to cry. "You're always making me feel bad," she accused. "Right from the start you raised your arms to Zeke and ran away from me. Soon as you could walk, you ran away from me, and you never wanted to cuddle the way the boys did when they were little. Sure, I get mad sometimes, but it's your own fault. You're the one."

"I can't help being the way I am, Ma," Shari said quietly.

"Yes, you can," Charlotte said. "If I can, you can too." She stood there and wiped away an overflow of tears with the back of her hand. Then she looked at Shari, who was watching her, trying to understand why Charlotte was crying. "You can take your bird back," Charlotte said. "I'm not about to do anything to harm it."

After lunch, Shari retrieved the crystal bird from its nesting place in her boot, wrapped it in a bandanna and tied it to the loop of her jeans. She told Peter she was going to visit Mrs. Wallace, and he asked to come along.

Charlotte was on the phone talking excitedly to BeeJay when Shari interrupted her to tell her where she and Peter were going. The hand with the cigarette tucked between the fingers waved her on.

"Like I say," Charlotte told BeeJay, "I could come in part time whenever you need me and handle the appointment book and the cash register, and—Sure why not?"

August heat lay heavily on them as they walked. It felt good to get into the shade of the dense woods. "When are we going to pan for gold again?" Peter asked.

"Tomorrow if you want," she said. The idea didn't attract her especially, but there were so few summer days left before school began. Then, she knew, Peter would be absorbed by the lively activities of his own age group and not so dependent on her for company.

When she returned to school, she planned to go to the library and read up on the air force and find out just how to go about making a career in the service. That her father had been a pilot was an omen. Even though he'd never really been her father, he'd left her a direction in the seed that was all he'd given of himself to Charlotte.

It would be good if Charlotte got a job and got out of the house more. It would be better for Shari if Charlotte got a job. She'd be less bored, and she had promised about Blue Boy. Shari was still mulling it over when she saw Mrs. Wallace standing on the bridge that spanned her pond, throwing out bread crumbs.

"Well, what a nice surprise to see you two," she called to them.

"What are you doing?" Peter asked.

"Feeding the fish. Look." She pointed to moving crescents that looked like chips of orange sunset in the water.

"Wow!" Peter said. "You got a lot of fish. Can I feed some?"

She handed him the plastic bag she was holding. "Be my guest," she said and turned to Shari. "Looks as if your little brother has recovered. How are you doing?"

"Fine," Shari said. "I came to make a trade with you, your crystal bird for Blue Boy."

"Oh, you want him back, do you? Think he's safe enough now?"

"I think so. Things are getting better. . . . I want to thank you for what you offered. You know, about me living with you? But I've decided to stay home with Zeke and Peter—and my mother."

"You and your mother doing better together?"

"I hope so. Maybe," Shari said.

"Good. That's very good news, and remember, I'll be here if you should need me any time."

"Oh, you'll be seeing a lot of me because of the bird banding," Shari said and added, "Also because you're my best friend, Mrs. Wallace."

Mrs. Wallace laughed and said, "That's an honour. I don't have too many friends I admire more than you, Shari."

The compliment embarrassed Shari, but it pleased her too. With Peter trailing behind, she followed Mrs. Wallace into the house to the big picture window in the living room where Blue Boy's cage hung. The parakeet hopped immediately onto the finger Shari extended to him. Then he ducked his head and blinked his eyes and chuckled at her rapidly as if he had a lot to tell her.

"I'm going to concentrate on teaching him to talk," Shari said. "I bet he'll learn fast."

"He's certainly a sociable fellow." Mrs. Wallace's face crinkled with amusement as she spoke.

"He likes to be with people just like Peter and my mother do," Shari said.

"Some creatures don't know how to enjoy their own company the way you and I do," Mrs. Wallace said.

"I enjoy a lot of things in life," Shari said. "I guess I'm pretty lucky."

"Are you?" Mrs. Wallace asked softly. "Well, perhaps you are. You've got the strength to fly free in the world, and it's a kind of luck to have that."

"Yes," Shari agreed. She stroked the blue-feathered head delicately with one finger, glad that her friend understood. Then she smiled as it came to her suddenly what it meant to be strong. She was free. Her fears could no longer cage her. One day, like the hawk, she would spread her wings and soar.

All these books are available at your local bookshop or newsagent, or can be ordered direct from the publisher. Indicate the number of copies required and fill in the form below.

Send to: **CS Department, Pan Books Ltd., P.O. Box 40, Basingstoke, Hants. RG21 2YT.**

or phone: 0256 469551 (Ansaphone), quoting title, author and Credit Card number.

Please enclose a remittance* to the value of the cover price plus: 60p for the first book plus 30p per copy for each additional book ordered to a maximum charge of £2.40 to cover postage and packing.

*Payment may be made in sterling by UK personal cheque, postal order, sterling draft or international money order, made payable to Pan Books Ltd.

Alternatively by Barclaycard/Access:

Card No. ☐☐☐☐☐☐☐☐☐☐☐☐☐☐☐☐

Signature:

Applicable only in the UK and Republic of Ireland.

While every effort is made to keep prices low, it is sometimes necessary to increase prices at short notice. Pan Books reserve the right to show on covers and charge new retail prices which may differ from those advertised in the text or elsewhere.

NAME AND ADDRESS IN BLOCK LETTERS PLEASE:

....

Name—————————————————————————

Address—————————————————————————

——————————————————————————————

——————————————————————————————

——————————————————————————————

3/87